Drachman's DILEMMAS

Drachman's Dilemmas
Copyright © 2024 by Thomas G. Livernois

Published in the United States of America

Library of Congress Control Number: 2024909341
ISBN   Paperback: 979-8-89091-549-8
ISBN   eBook: 979-8-89091-550-4

All rights reserved. No part of this publication may be reproduced, stored in a retrieval system or transmitted in any way by any means, electronic, mechanical, photocopy, recording or otherwise without the prior permission of the author except as provided by USA copyright law.

The opinions expressed by the author are not necessarily those of ReadersMagnet, LLC.

ReadersMagnet, LLC
10620 Treena Street, Suite 230
San Diego, California, 92131 USA
1.619. 354. 2643 | www.readersmagnet.com

Book design copyright © 2024 by ReadersMagnet, LLC. All rights reserved.

Cover design by Jhiee Oraiz
Interior design by Don De Guzman

Drachman's DILEMMAS

THOMAS G. LIVERNOIS

CHAPTER ONE

> There are enough industrialists and too many scientists, but compared to mathematicians and lawyers, irrespectively, the world is left wanting.
>
> Wellsley Swiston

I hastily opened the package that Andy had just delivered and read the bottom line. It was good news. The electromagnetic compatibility (EMC) test correlation report from General Motors' Kokomo, Indiana electronics lab arrived two weeks later than promised via UPS overnight.

The comparison data I had supplied agreed very well with their results! Although I had already done some work for one of GM's anti-lock brake (ABS) suppliers, I was trying (now successfully) to demonstrate that my company, Forward Research and Test, could also provide repeatable, cost-effective test services for pre- and post-production radio products built in Kokomo. The best part was that even though the uncertainties in my test stand calibrations were given as worst case in this initial report, I still had room to spare. I would be getting a lot of business now!

Goals: if you reach them, don't raise them. Don't. That's what I say.

"Thanks Andy," I said. Andy Brooks was my only employee and most trusted friend.

"Right. Any outgoing?" He asked. Andy was also a Korean War veteran and recipient of the Purple Heart. In addition to being a top notch EMC technician, he did the odd jobs around the office: bathroom, windows, and every day just after lunch, mail. Prior to joining my company, after a stint in the 1950s military, he was a civilian employee of the Air Force. He was many things.

"No," I said, "just incoming" Why pay fifteen bucks for overnight mail when the information in it is already fourteen days late? Because the status of my company's business goals for General Motors, my primary client, depended on the results in that report.

The phone rang and I considered letting the voice mail get it, but then picked it up. I love to answer the phone. It's like an estate sale. You never know what you'll find.

"Forward Research and Test, Frank Drachman," I answered.

"Mr. Drachman, this is Detective Carmichael of the Dearborn Police Department," the tired, methodical voice replied.

I knew immediately that this call was about my confrontation with that British prick yesterday in the main outer hallway of the Ford Design Center. It happened after a meeting of the American

Automobile Manufacturers Association (AAMA), an industry lobby group that attempts to get the Big Three and their suppliers to work effectively together in certain areas, so that they can better compete in the world market. This translates to beating the Japanese and the Germans. The Japanese are still harder to beat and there is no need to worry about the French and the British, but keep an eye on the Germans.

I represented GM through my own company, Forward Research and Test, a small, second tier outfit that does no research and, hopefully, lots of mundane compliance testing. An executive engineer at GM, Burt Morgan, offered me a blanket contract to participate in the name of General Motors with this AAMA subcommittee, which deals with international product EMC testing. I said yes. Meetings are held at different locations each month. The contract also came with an invitation to prove competence in electromagnetic compatibility testing, with the added caveat of substantial future test business. Yesterday's meeting was held at the Ford Design Center in Dearborn. And that's where I was.

"What can I do for you, Detective?"

"Can you come down to the station today, this afternoon, to answer a few questions?" He asked.

"Well, I guess so, but what's this about?" I asked, playing dumb.

"Routine questioning. Do you know Ian Hatley?"

"I don't think so, what happened?"

"According to Ford security, yesterday afternoon you allegedly punched him in the nose at their Design Center."

"That could be true," I confessed. "But I didn't know him otherwise."

"Well enough," replied the detective, "I'm on duty until seven. Can you come down to headquarters sometime tonight?"

"I guess so. Do I need a lawyer?"

"I doubt it. But, of course, that's up to you. I just have a few questions to ask."

When I left my lab in Madison Heights (blue collar suburb of Detroit), I didn't think too much about being questioned until rush hour traffic slowed me to a stop on the Southfield Freeway. Then I wondered if I should have brought a lawyer. Nah. What could happen? I continued south on the Southfield, as we call it here in the motor city, and took the Michigan Avenue east exit. Ten minutes later I pulled into the visitor parking lot at the Dearborn Police Station. They never tell you to bring a lawyer, or even that you may need one, and on this occasion I probably should have had one. But I was tired of lawyers.

The front entrance to the station had modern, tinted glass doors and a simulated marble floor. It led straight to a desk attended by either a rookie or a guy that drew the short straw this month. There are times when you can just look at someone you've never seen before and tell that he hates what he's doing. This guy had that look. I regarded him informally.

"Is Detective Carmichael in? I have an appointment."

"What's your name?" He asked.

"Drachman. Frank Drachman."

"Is that German?"

"No, that's my name," I told him. My confidence was high.

Good news from General Motors goes a long way. He didn't get it. I had attempted a joke, albeit a bad one, at the wrong time, but this guy was an over serious, uptight fellow. I asked him if he was the receptionist. He wasn't. Hopefully, Detective Carmichael was not so conservative. But if he was, it made sense. Police work was serious; therefore, police officers were serious, right?

"Why don't you have a seat and I'll call him," he told me.

"Thank you."

I sat down on a new, many-shades-of-brown lobby couch that someone must have gotten a deal on and looked at the latest *Newsweek* magazine. I also checked my watch several times: 6.21, 6.24. Ten minutes passed. Detective Carmichael came out.

He was a cross between Banecek and Cannon - a corpulent man who wore all the wrong clothes. He wore a size fifteen shirt and had a size seventeen neck. A case study of don't for GQ.

Right behind him was Ed Finninen, a colleague of mine from Ford who I worked with on the AAMA subcommittee. Ed and I went to school together a dozen years ago at Michigan Tech, in the Eli Whitney

School of Engineering, but we didn't know each other then. We met in the auto world. He was a mechanical engineer, I was electrical - volts and newtons don't always mix. There was hope for Ed though. He laughed when I told him that the only thing a mechanical engineer needed to know was that you can't push on a rope. But today Ed didn't look happy. And what the hell was he doing at the police station?

"Hey Ed, what's going on here?" I asked.

"Frank, hello. Some guy from England got beat up pretty bad last night. He's at Oakwood Hospital in Dearborn. They don't know if he's going to make it."

"Are you Frank Drachman?" The detective asked me.

"Yes," I replied. "See you at the next meeting," I told Ed.

"Right," he said, then left the building.

"Detective Carmichael?" I asked. "I'm here to answer some questions, I guess, about Ian Hatley."

"Yes, thanks for coming down. Did you bring a lawyer?"

"No. I'm here by myself."

"Do you want a cup of coffee?" He asked.

"No thanks. Beaned out for the day."

"What?" He was puzzled.

"Nothing." It was going to be a long night.

He nodded in the direction of a yellowish, nicotine-stained hallway littered with no smoking signs. This place was stuck. The walls needed paint, an update to today. The detective and I started down the hall together, but I moved faster than he did and had to regularly slow down so he could catch up. Invariably I sped up again and then had to slow down to wait for him. He did it intentionally.

The station looked much larger inside than outside, so Detective Carmichael was well suited for this building. At the end of the hall, maybe thirty steps from the lobby, we turned left and then quickly left again into a small questioning room. He instructed me to take a seat, then sat down himself and opened the spiral notepad that was already on the table next to a telephone.

Except for my red shirt and Detective Carmichael's Loony Tunes necktie, everything in the room was black, white or some shade of gray. Someone looking in the door could easily have mistaken the scene for a magazine advertisement for men's apparel: *Wear these clothes, be noticed!* it would say.

We were seated on opposite sides of the table. Detective Carmichael dialed the phone, paused, grunted; he may even have farted - he was one of those noisy people - then hung up. About five minutes later, another police officer, a very attractive, dark-haired woman officer, with just a little extra weight on her hips and butt, joined us. She looked awkward in the blue uniform, which smelled like cigarette smoke, but she moved smoothly, like a luxury car. I felt a throb of excitement. What do these people want with me?

"Mr. Drachman, this is Officer Munday. She's been assigned to the case with me."

"How do you do, Officer?" I said, half standing to shake her hand.

"Fine, thanks. Don't get up," she replied in a focused, raspy voice.

"I'll bet," I said, knowing the answer, "that this has to do with the altercation I was in yesterday at the Ford Design Center. I thought Ford security would handle it."

"They are involved," said Officer Munday, "but the Design Center is in Dearborn, so we have ultimate jurisdiction."

Then Detective Carmichael added, "Ian Hatley was found all but beaten to death near a dumpster at Fairlane Mall this morning. He's at Oakwood Hospital in critical condition, and they don't know if he's going to make it. We estimate that he was attacked at about midnight. If this were December instead of June, he would have frozen to death. Basically, he is very lucky to be alive."

When he said midnight, I thought about my alibi. And then I wondered why people say things like: he is lucky to be alive. Why not say: he is unlucky to have been pounded to shit? I'll bet Ian Hatley doesn't feel lucky.

"What does that have to do with me?" I inquired. "I was with someone from about eight o'clock last night until six this morning - Cindy Salome. She works with me on the AAMA subcommittee."

"With those hours, it doesn't sound like business. Besides, that doesn't mean you weren't involved," said Detective Carmichael

"Well, I know that I wasn't. But, ah, then let's go through it." I was getting nervous. Do they think I hired somebody to put Ian Hatley in the hospital? I decided to tell them the truth…

I had just spent two hours in a warm, cramped meeting room with about a dozen AAMA representatives from Ford, Chrysler and several electrical parts suppliers. We were trying to work out an agreement on how to share enough information on several electromagnetic compatibility test procedures without giving away too much. This stuff isn't top secret rocket science, but we all liked to think so. Remember, you're only as important as what you do. An important charter of the AAMA was to get the Big Three and their suppliers to agree on technical issues pertaining to overseas vehicle sales. This way, if all the American companies are on one side, it makes them all more formidable. As if General Motors needed help!

The meeting did not go very well. I was overruled by committee majority on a couple of points. It was frustrating. I left conference room 2B cranky. Just outside the conference room, within the well-lit and modern secured area of the Design Center, there is a hallway that leads to the lobby, which, to get to, requires passing through doors that need an access card. Authorized visitors obtained their passes from the receptionist in the lobby.

So I'm walking down this hallway after the meeting and the now identified Ian Hatley is coming in from the lobby. I saw him swipe his card through the reader. He started walking confidently in my direction. He appeared not to recognize me, but I suddenly knew that he was the drunk who broke my nose two months ago.

At that time, it was a Friday night, I was on my way to Metro Airport to pick up my wife Beth. She was scheduled to land at nine o'clock. I decided to stop at Friday's at Fairlane Mall for a beer. I left work at six; it was on the way; there was time to kill. The parking lot was overflowing with Ford products. The place was packed like a sardine can.

I worked my way in and was standing there at the bar in my new topcoat drinking a Budweiser. Then Lisa Brooks, a friend who worked at Ford that I had met through my wife, walks by unexpectedly. We say hi, hug and start small talking. About two minutes later, this group of drunken, drawling Brits stumble into me and I spill my beer. Everything is "brilliant" to the drunken English. I pushed back, and the next thing I know, this Ian Hatley character is in my face pointing at my chest. I don't know exactly what he said, but it was along the lines of: We have to fight now because you pushed me back and in a crowded bar you should expect to spill your beer: Naturally, as with all drunks, there must have been some kind of logic to what he said, but it went beyond me. I was thinking to myself, why me? Why now? Between his slurred speech and his accent, I could not understand him very well. I smiled, laughed, and told him to lighten up and watch where you're going, then turned back to Lisa and our discussion about Ronald Reagan's case of Alzheimer's. We were in the process of concluding that it was comforting to know that during those Iran-contra hearings, he really didn't remember.

Out of nowhere, this drunk spins me around and headbutts me right on the bridge of my nose. By the time my eyes stopped watering either the bouncer or the guy's friends had dragged him off: I did not see him again that night - lucky for him. There was a cut and a bump where he made contact. Must be a soccer player, I thought. The bleeding stopped with the help of ice; I sardonically proclaimed myself HIV negative in case that the slightly concerned surrounding patrons were wondering. My adrenaline was peaked. The night was ruined. I looked around the bar, said goodnight to Lisa and left.

During the drive to the airport I calmed down a little. I picked up Beth in front of the Northwest Airlines terminal, severely cutting off a US park shuttle in the process. Of course, she had to know why my nose was swollen, so I explained it. Most of the time women don't understand why men fight. This was no exception. We drove home, watched a little TV, then really messed up the bed - we hadn't seen each other in three days.

Saturday morning, I went for a long run and made the fine decision to put it all behind me. It was the weekend. No point in dwelling on Friday; Monday was just around the corner. That's how it went two months ago.

When I unexpectedly saw him yesterday at the Design Center walking confidently in my direction, my blood boiled.

I'd swear he had a smirk on his face. I saw red. I'll admit I'm one to project anger, that my therapies had limits, but it was a bad meeting and this guy had it coming. I was suddenly, strangely, enraged. It happened all by itself, as if I, Frank Drachman, was along only for the ride. One minute I was a little grouchy, the next minute I was flaming mad!

Tactically, however, it was very useful that he appeared not to recognize me. Since he's British, he walked on the left side of the hall (from his perspective) and we were walking right at each other. When I was about ten feet from him, I covertly switched my briefcase from my left hand to my right hand. Without blinking or thinking, I clenched my fist hard, cocked my left arm, and popped him square in the face, really hard. He had no idea what happened. Just like me in the bar.

He stumbled backwards and fell on his butt. It was a good shot. Blood began to slowly seep out of both nostrils. I don't think that I've ever hit anyone so well. He deserved it, he did break my nose. I told him never to headbutt a stranger, then I walked briskly toward the lobby, finally able to appreciate the brewing potential for trouble.

I finished up my story to the police by quantifying the amount of time associated with the Design Center event.

"This all happened in about ten seconds, but since I didn't plan to hit him, I didn't have an escape plan or anything. Afterwards, I walked, switched the briefcase back to my left hand, swiped the visitor's access card through the reader, passed through the doors and returned the card to the receptionist. By the time security arrived, I was in my car, driving. That's how it happened. I have not seen him since advising him not to headbutt strangers. I assumed that Ford security would figure out who I was."

"Are there any witnesses who saw what happened at Friday's?" Asked Detective Carmichael.

"Yes," I said, "Lisa Brooks, for one, the bartender maybe. I'm not sure. It happened very quickly, and it was two months ago too. What does it matter anyway?"

"It will help us confirm Mr. Hatley's identity," said Officer Munday.

"I thought you already knew who he was."

"We do know that the man in Oakwood Hospital is Ian Hatley and that you punched him yesterday. What we do not know is whether or not he is the same man who attacked you two months ago," she said.

"Well, I'm telling you, just like I'm planning to tell Ford security, he is the same person." The two officers looked at each other, unconvinced.

Then Officer Munday asked me, "Do you know of any reason why Mr. Hatley might be following you?"

"No. Why would he follow me? I supply test services for a car company's suppliers. All I do is test automobile parts. That's it, nothing more. Until I saw him in that hallway, I hadn't thought about him in two months. Sure, I was surprised at how angry it made me to see him, but I don't just hit people in the face unless they deserve it."

"If you were to see him now," said Detective Carmichael, "you'd understand that your punch in the nose is the least of his problems."

Then Officer Munday added, "We don't know Mr. Hatley's motives either. One possible reason that he was following you, and I'm speculating, is that you have something he wants. He may even have been after Ed Finninen."

"I don't understand why he would follow me, or Ed for that matter. Ed is the son of a pastie chef from Ishpeming. Is this some sort of industrial espionage or what? We're test engineers with nothing to hide. The people in body styling and powertrain planning, they have the biggest secrets. All I do is make sure the final product is legal to sell. There's no creativity or innovation, just procedure and compliance."

Officer Munday was taking notes rapidly.

I then asked for a cup of coffee, black.

Detective Carmichael went to get it. Times have changed.

Officer Munday stopped writing and looked at me, straight in the eyes. "Do you mind if I smoke?"

"No, I guess not. Do I make you nervous?" I couldn't help flirting. She had blue eyes and black hair and I wondered about her.

"You're cute, but I'm gay, so don't bother."

"But haven't you heard that bisexuality is in? I just read about it in your *Newsweek* magazine."

She looked at me blankly. Very stern. This was a serious woman who had only business on her mind.

As she lit up, I responded. "Okay, well, what else do we need to discuss?"

Detective Carmichael came in and set a cup of black coffee on the table in front of me. "There you are Mr. Drachman," he said.

"Thanks." I smelled the coffee and cigarette smoke and noticed again my black and white surroundings. I felt like Richard Kimble in an early episode of *The Fugitive*. Then I just had to say it out loud: "For what it's worth, I didn't do it." What was wrong with me? Ever since I'd separated from Beth, I tended to blurt things out, like I was trying to make up for things I hadn't said. She wouldn't have listened, but still, to say them is important.

"Didn't do what, Mr. Drachman?" asked Detective Carmichael.

"Whatever it is you think I did, besides hitting Ian Hatley in the nose in the Design Center yesterday."

The officers looked at each other, eyebrows raised.

"You are a strange man, Mr. Drachman. Can I see your hands?" Asked Officer Munday.

I set the coffee cup in my left hand down and then stretched out both arms.

She took my left hand first and pressed her thumbs between the middle knuckles where it was still swollen from hitting Ian Hatley. Then she observed and felt my right hand similarly. "You hit him hard."

"Yes, I did. But I still have a bump on my nose from him. See?" I took her hand and rubbed her forefinger back and forth over the bump, several times.

"How many times?" She asked me, while ignoring that last part by professionally pulling away her hand.

"I told you; I punched him one time in the nose - eye for an eye, and I'm not even religious; it's just a good way to be."

"He does have a broken nose. But he's in critical condition because someone broke six of his ribs and punctured his lung. His spleen is ruptured too. Lots of internal bleeding." These qualifications she read from her notebook, flipping pages back and forth.

"You don't think I had anything to do with last night, do you?" I asked, before Detective Carmichael could interrupt.

"Well, if you were with this Cindy Salome, you certainly couldn't have done it without some help. How can we get in touch with her to verify your location last night?"

I gave him Cindy's work phone.

The next part is where having a lawyer with me would have helped. The lawyer would have said something like, either press charges right now or release my client. Instead, I chose the stoic approach: assault with intent to kill is a serious crime.

"It sounds like you're assuming I'm guilty. Well, I didn't do it!" I exclaimed. "I'm perfectly willing to take responsibility for the incident yesterday at the Design Center. In fact, I'm going to call Ford security tomorrow and tell them everything. How could I have known that some dipshit Brit from two months ago worked in the Design Center, and that I would pass him in an empty hallway? How could I not hit him? Even though revenge is sweet, I'm no killer!"

"That makes some sense, Mr. Drachman, but there is another problem," said Officer Munday, finishing an exhale. She was very erotic, like Sean Young in *Bladerunner*, with that cigarette smoke curling out of her nose.

Detective Carmichael watched her too.

"What problem?"

"Nobody knows what Mr. Hatley was doing in the Design Center. He doesn't work for Ford, or for any supplier," she explained.

I looked intently at her eyebrows and the experienced wrinkles at the corners of her eyes.

"Furthermore, Mr. Hatley didn't call security after you assaulted him. He evidently didn't want anyone to know he was there. A secretary from one of the offices lining the hallway witnessed the event and notified security. Mr. Hatley left the building, using Ed Finninen's badge, long before security personnel arrived. Ed Finninen recalled bumping into Mr. Hatley in the lobby after the AAMA meeting. We believe that Mr. Hatley pickpocketed Mr. Finninen at that time because we found Ed Finninen's badge on Mr. Hatley this morning."

I thought of Columbo and how he used to tell the prime suspect everything he knew. It felt bad. I also remembered that Ed left the meeting sooner than I did, enabling him to get to the lobby first.

"Now do you understand, Mr. Drachman?" Asked Detective Carmichael.

"I think so. But I want to call a lawyer, now."

"No need for that," said Officer Munday. "You can go now. But don't leave the Detroit area until we've cleared up some things and confirmed that you were with Cindy Salome last night. Whether or not Mr. Hatley will press assault charges against you remains to be seen, but you better hope that when, or if, he wakes up, he doesn't implicate you further. Cindy Salome wouldn't be the first woman to lie for a man."

I drove home to my unpacked apartment and called Cindy. She picked up before the first ring ended. Expect a call from the Dearborn Police, I told her. Naturally, she was full of questions.

"Why did you have to hit him and make yourself a suspect? Why couldn't you just let it go? Did you pay somebody to do it?" A sinister mind for such a sweet girl. She always asked questions that I couldn't answer very well. Goodnight.

I mixed up a tall Rob Roy, drank it too fast, and tumbled into bed to watch TV. My old friend TV.

CHAPTER TWO

And hope?
That vast shadow, testing and fading into
the past.
For which there is no quarter?
For it must be.
And why?

> Hugo S. Blackmeer

The next morning, I awoke quickly. Wednesday. Shit! I had an 8.00 A.M. meeting with Burt Morgan, and it was already 7.30 A.M. There was absolutely no way to get dressed and drive from my Novi apartment to his office at the GM Tech Center in Warren in thirty minutes! I located the cordless phone, then remembered that I did not have Burt Morgan's phone number memorized. And I had left my Franklin planner at the lab. It was true: I could not function effectively without it. Just as they claimed in the *'How to use a Franklin planner'* class. Damn.

First the AT&T operator, then the switchboard at the GM Tech Center. Finally, his phone was ringing. It answered, "You have reached the office of Burt Morgan. Mr. Morgan is not in at the present time, so please leave your name and number and a short message. He will return your call as soon as possible." Annie, his executive assistant (secretary), had a pretty voice. *Beep.*

"Burt, Frank Drachman. I'm running late. Very sorry. I should be in your office by eight-thirty, no later. I hope it's not a huge problem. Very sorry. I'm home right now, leaving in fifteen minutes." Too often my messages sounded like riot-zone cable transmissions for the Associated Press. Hardly any extra words.

This, of course, was not the way to get repeat business with the largest corporation the world has ever seen. But there was nothing I could do about it. I proceed to the shower and the phone rang just as the water approached the right temperature. I answered naked.

"Hello, this is Frank Drachman."

"Frank, Burt Morgan. I guess this caller ID really works. Say, Frank, no need to meet this morning."

My heart sank. "All right Burt. I am really very sorry about— "

"Don't worry about it, Frank", he interrupted. "But can you be in Tucson by two o'clock mountain time today?"

I envisioned Detective Carmichael and Officer Munday looking at me nodding nope. Without hesitation, I replied, "Absolutely. What do you need?" Here was a chance to save face.

"Well, the anti-lock brake modules that Bagelle Braking supplies for our large pickup trucks are failing during vehicle prove-outs at the test track. Bagelle claims that you did all of the proper subsystem validation tests before they released the design for production. They claim that they tested and passed samples from the first production build at their lab in Tucson. I'm not sure I believe that, and I need you to go out there again and see what they are not doing. See what tests they're screwing up."

"Okay, Burt. I'll call you tonight. Do they know I'm coming?"

"Yes. Call Faqualal?"

"Right." I felt a knot tightening in my stomach. How could I tell Burt Morgan that I could not be on call (the main reason he wanted me set up with a blanket contract) because I was now a potential assault with intent to kill suspect? I simply had to go. I stopped at the lab to get my planner and Bagelle test documentation, then on the way to the airport, I hit a McDonald's drive-thru for a large coffee and an egg something or other.

The engineer at Bagelle Braking referred to by Burt Morgan was Habib Faqualal, a pretty smart guy from Iraq who got out just in time. He always took me to this restaurant near the airport in Phoenix called Feast on Halal. Since meeting Habib, I had come to learn that Halal is a term reserved for meat that is prepared by saying a prayer before and after killing the animal. Beef, poultry, and lamb, I think, are acceptable folder for this ceremony. The way Habib explained it sounded kosher, just a different religion. Finer salt — no difference in taste. So, if you are with a Muslim friend who plays by the rules, make sure the meat is Halal meat. But unless you were there, how would you know if somebody said a prayer? I didn't go into this with Habib. It all reminded me of when I would tell Beth that the ice cream I bought was fat-free yogurt. She always felt better and never got fat. You see my point. Overall, the holy meat, service, atmosphere, and prices at Feast on Halal were quite agreeable. I enjoyed every meal I had eaten there. I was used to the valet parking at Detroit Metro Airport and found my way onto the fight to Phoenix. From there I'd drive to Tucson.

Since there was a big problem with Habib's product, he knew someone representing General Motors would be out to Arizona soon. After another breakfast, I decided to call him from the jet using the credit card phone on the back of the seat in front of me, while *Fern Gully* played on the video screen directly above my head. I had an aisle seat too close to the screen. I consulted my Franklin planner, confidently, for Habib's number. I dialed it. Although it was still early in Tucson, Habib answered on the third ring.

"Hello, this is Habib Faqualal," he answered elegantly.

I found his Middle Eastern accent very soothing. "Hi Habib, this is Frank Drachman. Burt Morgan asked me to come out and review Bagelle's survivability tests for the large GM truck ABS module."

"Fine, I—" he tried.

"I'm on a plane as we speak, somewhere, I'd guess, over Oklahoma. I'll be in Arizona in a few hours." The coffee had kicked in. I could no longer listen well, and had the urge to speak quickly.

"Fine, I—"

"We need to review everything. Burt is contemplating a plant shutdown in St. Louis."

"A plant shutdown. Oh no!" cried Habib. Being responsible for a plant shutdown in the auto business is like being given three months to live; there's always a good, solid, understandable reason. And you're still fucked. Habib knew this.

"What about shutting down the other plant, the one in Brazil?" he asked.

"Not right now," I told him.

"Are they not the same vehicle?"

"Yes, essentially. But that's Burt's call, Habib. We need to find the root cause."

Why keep building cars that may need to be fixed before they're even sold? Why? Because people buy them. Now, contrary to what people may think, if a legitimate safety issue exists, the plants are stopped. For the present Bagelle ABS module, the problem was reported by the proving ground drivers as an intermittent loss of ABS functionality at speeds less than 20 mph. The regular, or foundation, brakes were fine. Not good, but not deadly.

"Frank," Habib said solemnly, "would you like me to pick you up from the airport?"

"I suppose it would save time. What kind of car will you be driving?"

"I only know it will be a General Motors product. Look for your name on a small poster board."

"Okay, thanks. My flight is Northwest 257." I wanted to say North by Northwest in honor of Alfred Hitchcock, but held it in.

"I shall see you soon, Frank"

Habib picked me up at terminal three of the Sky Harbor Airport in a green Grand Prix with a sign in his hand and a frown on his face. We drove to the Bagelle engineering and manufacturing plant, between Phoenix and Tucson, but closer to Tucson, just off of 1-10. I forced myself not to think about the Dearborn Police Department, except for Officer Munday. I couldn't help it. I tried to concentrate on the desolate Arizona landscape, and reminisced about the coyote and the roadrunner. I felt like a dead, miserable tumbleweed blowing where I was blown. You cannot argue with the wind; it won't listen to your side of the story. We arrived one hour after I got into Habib's company car.

We entered the test lab through a back entrance and drew the confined attention of the technician and engineers who worked there with Habib. It was the closest thing to fame that I had ever experienced. They all looked somberly at us, me. I wondered what it would be like to live the life of Lee Iacocca. After the Tracinda debacle, so did Lee.

There were several tests set up and ready to go. We went through all of them, checked each calibration, discussed every conceivable oversight. Nothing. I made the Bagelle crew do every one, beginning to end. Twice. No luck. The modules were performing exactly as they should. Damn. I had just spent a whole day learning nothing. One of many.

If the module was not the problem, what then? Maybe they were installing it wrong at the assembly plant. Maybe the vehicle test evaluated something that the module test did not. Maybe the driver was imagining things. I needed to see Burt Morgan. He'd know what to do. The only flight back to Detroit was a red-eye, so Habib and I would eat supper together at Feast on Halal.

We drove for over an hour on 1-10 for an hour back to Phoenix and exited onto 16th Street. Habib wheeled the Grand Prix into the parking lot. He really looked forward to eating here, especially since it was on Bagelle Braking. Business is business. I suspected that Habib did not get out much.

We were seated in a booth, next to a mini-jukebox and speaker that wrestled out Middle Eastern music. Habib ordered the Halal Grande. It was specially seasoned lamb and chicken served over seasoned couscous. What came first, the chicken or the lamb? I decided to try the Herder's Feast. Lamb, what else? It was served with potatoes and some vegetable smothered in oil. We both ordered without looking up from the menu.

Habib and I didn't ever talk much. He was a genuine man of few words. I was a man of too many words, lately. A silent combination. Ten minutes had passed. We were quiet because we did not know who to blame for the Bagelle ABS module problems. The music struggled. Finally, our dinner came.

"Frank," he began, after I had just taken a bite, "how is your wife?"

"Habib, I have no idea," I replied blankly. I had embarrassed him.

He looked firmly at his food and tore off a piece of meat that had several pieces of Israeli couscous stuck to it.

"Habib, Beth and I are getting a divorce."

"Frank, I am sorry to hear this."

"Part of me is, too, Habib. But when it's over, it's over."

He was quiet, respectful. It's awkward hearing somebody you know, but not very well, talk about personal problems.

I changed the subject. "So how is your wife?"

"Sushil is wonderful." He lit right up. "She is carrying. Seven months now."

"Well, congratulations!" I responded mechanically. "How many little Habibs are there again?"

"We have only one boy, Bashar. Sushil is hoping for a little girl."

"What name will you call her?"

"I prefer Melinda. Sushil likes Teresa. We do not know how it will turn out."

"What about if you get a boy?"

"Sushil is very firm on William. I think William is fine."

Habib and Sushil were adjusting well to life in America.

"All of those names sound just right to me, Habib."

"Thank you, Frank."

Dinner with Habib further confused the difficulty I had with formal men. We finished eating and left Feast on Halal. The airport was only five minutes away and Habib began to slow to drop me off right where he picked me up.

"Thank you for everything, Frank. Please tell me if there is anything, anything at all, that I can do to improve the situation."

"I sure will, Habib. Thanks for dinner and the ride. You don't need to stop. I'll just jump out and tuck and roll." Habib looked quite concerned until he realized I had made a joke and came to a gradual stop. He smiled. Perhaps there was hope! I took my Franklin planner and valise from the back seat, climbed out, and slammed shut the green door. The airport was pretty empty. The south-western theme was apparent.

Several doors and two escalators later, at the Northwest terminal (I forget the number), I realized there were two choices: drink coffee and try to stay awake, or drink alcohol and try to go to sleep. It was four hours until my flight left, so I decided slowly. I was good at that.

The lamb was causing me discomfort. I decided to sit at a malodorous table in an airport lounge and watch *Jeopardy*. Here, for a mere three dollars, you could buy fourteen ounces of lukewarm Budweiser.

There was an *Inc.* magazine lying on the table next to me, so I picked it up. Page after page of how Joe (or Jane) Blo made a quarter of a million per year at some Fortune 500 company, but just had to quit because he (or she) had to be his (or her) own boss. Now he (or she) makes two and a half million a year. What was I doing wrong? GM paid me one thousand dollars per day, plus expenses, regardless of how many hours I worked. Two and a half million a year translated to just under seven thousand per day! I would have to talk Burt Morgan.

I read on and came across a Rolex advertisement that featured Jean-Claude Killy, the Olympic skier. He was pictured at the top of the page, high in some set of lovely, snow-covered mountains, wearing a nice sweater and a smile. At the bottom of the page was a picture of the famous Rolex watch. In the middle of the page, he was quoted as saying: "I don't think I'll ever slow down." I thought about it for a minute. Let me see, Olympic medal twenty or thirty years ago, still living off of it. That's capitalism, isn't it? I concluded that Jean-Claude had slowed down. We all do. He just didn't know it yet.

When I was eighteen my grandmother told me, "You live and you die, and in between you work." She was right. Working kept the carrot of contentment just out of my reach. And you could never work enough to change the ending. I knew this. But it did keep me focused on all kinds of material things, including spirituality. That French intellectual, Bertran de Jouvenel, took fifteen pages (of mostly bullshit) to explain that a successful capitalistic economy requires that most of the people in it are rarely happy. Otherwise, how can you get them to buy anything? Happy people don't want to but things they can't afford, except food, and there's plenty of that in America, regardless of what you hear. How much additional rubble do we really need? Thinking about these things overwhelmed me. I was a test engineer, not a philosopher.

I must have fallen asleep. Suddenly my flight was making its final boarding call. Thank God I woke up. It would be easy now to get back home, as though I'd never left, and tend to things. Along with my baggage, I was herded onto the plane. I ended up in an aisle seat. There was a sleepy old man in the window seat to my right and another soldier of capitalism across the aisle to my left. I didn't notice anyone else.

The takeoff was nerve-racking. At Sky Harbor Airport there are only east-west runways. Unfortunately, on that day, there was a stiff wind from the north. We taxied, accelerated, and the nose of the aircraft lifted. As soon as the rear wheels left the ground, the Boeing 757 shifted hard to the right and bounced deep like it hit a huge, deep chuck hole. I almost pissed my pants. Flying, to begin with, was no favorite of mine.

After getting through the clouds, the ride became smooth. Soon, drinks were served. Scotch and water here. I was feeling pretty good. I had managed to satisfy my job requirements and disobey legal advice from the Dearborn Police Department in less than one day. Late Wednesday night on a plane. I decided to check my messages at home. And, admittedly, it was fun to use the credit card phone.

I dialed. The machine answered after three rings. I hit *5, followed by the secret code number, 205. I lead an exciting life. There were three new messages. The first was from Officer Munday.

"Mr. Drachman, this is Officer Munday from the Dearborn Police Department. We had a little surprise today at Oakwood Hospital. It seems that Ian Hatley woke up for about twenty seconds while a nurse was bathing him, and spoke only your name… (What? I Could not believe what I was hearing. How could he know my name?) … so, I need for you to come down to the station right away to clear up some more loose ends. The doctors don't know what to think. Oh yes, one more thing, if you get this message first, Detective Carmichael has left one on your office phone. Goodbye." *Click. Beep.* She probably smoked a cigarette after that message. She sounded agitated. Whenever she entered my mind, she never left it without my thinking about her piercing blue eyes and jet-black eyebrows. It was a striking combination. With that over, I was completely stunned by message two. It was even worse. It was from an absolutely frantic Cindy Salome.

"Frank, it's me. You are in big trouble. Ian Hatley died and they think you killed him! I just got another call from Detective Carmichael. He wanted to know where you were. I told him I didn't know. Call me when you get in. I'm really worried about you, Frank. I love you." There were two things in her message I had trouble with. We had agreed to a non-committal type relationship. Neither of our divorces were even final. Then it really hit me – Ian Hatley dead? I was screwed. Officer Munday left the third message.

"Mr. Drachman, this is Officer Munday. You need to come down to the station immediately." Her not telling me about his demise was a bad sign and I knew it was true. The Dearborn Police wanted to arrest me for the death of Ian Hatley! I no longer enjoyed using credit card phones on jetliners.

If I would have programmed that damned answering machine to attach the time to the end of each message, I would have had a better understanding of the day's events. But it was purchased at an estate sale in West Bloomfield a few months ago along with some furniture and a laptop computer. To save money, Beth and I decided to temporarily outfit an office in the basement with used accessories. No instructions were included with anything and there hadn't been time to play with the buttons to figure out the programming features of the answering machine. I took the office stuff with me when I moved out three weeks ago. Most of the boxes in my apartment weren't even unpacked.

So there I was, somewhere over Oklahoma again, in the middle of the night. The Dearborn Police Department wanted to charge me with murder, and I wanted to date one of my accusers, but she was gay. They were probably waiting, warrants in hand, outside my apartment door, or at my office, or at the airport. Do judges sign multiple copies of arrest warrants so that police at all stake-out locations have the paperwork necessary to legally ensnare the villain? Or do photocopies suffice? Me, the villain? What was happening? I was an underpaid test engineer with a used computer. I wondered how much of this was divorce related.

There were two options: go directly to the police station or run. It required a review. I had attacked Ian Hatley the day before he wound up in the hospital. The only thing he said before he died was my full name.

I imagined the trial. For some reason, I'd end up with the lawyer that the Joe Pesci character in *My Cousin Vinny* was based on. Was I a yute? Lie detector tests weren't admissible. And since I was not famous, there was no way that I'd have the same luck that O.J. Simpson did. I concluded, after my third scotch and water, that running was the answer. Maybe the Juice could loan me his disguise.

Norman Mailer wrote somewhere in *Harlot's Ghost* that if you drink scotch then you've given up. Well not me. I was just getting started. I had divorce to finish and a business to run. How to actually do these things as an outlaw had not occurred to me at that moment. With the decision made, it was time to celebrate.

"Waitress, another, thank you!" I demanded. Soon, the captain would be out, explaining how disorderly conduct aboard an aircraft was a felony. Felony. Ha! The flight attendant approached me.

"Are you quite sure, sir?" she asked tightly.

I wanted to set her up with the receptionist at the Dearborn Police Department. "When are we going to land?" I asked.

She checked her watch. "In about an hour, sir."

"I suppose I'll need my faculties to make it on the run."

"Pardon me?"

"No. I guess I'm all set. Thanks."

Deep down, I knew that when the plane landed at 6.00 A.M., I would go directly to the Dearborn Police Department, turn myself in to Officer Munday, and call my level-headed divorce lawyer, Ben David Fisher. He was the only lawyer I trusted. He worked at a good firm and could help me find a defense attorney. Ben always told me that I could call him anytime, day or night, but the rates might vary.

Besides, I didn't have the balls to run. I never did anything. Even Beth didn't believe me when I told her I wanted a divorce, I simply didn't love her. Why couldn't she get it? Until three weeks ago, when I stacked box after box of my things in the living room and waited at the kitchen table for the movers, she didn't think that I'd leave. She must have been astonished when she arrived home and found me gone. The next day she checked herself into the mental hospital in New Boston and stayed for a week. That's a stress leave. But she'd be fine when she found someone who couldn't make her happy and didn't care.

I did not want to use the on-board phone again – it only brought me bad news. So I decided to wait and call Ben David from the police station in a couple of hours. By then the sun would be up, and I'd save a few bucks. Play it by the books. Justice works. I fell asleep only to wake up with my head filled with thoughts of Johnie Cochran in a knit cap. The jet was circling Detroit Metro, preparing to land. I felt rotten and my head hurt. One too many. Did I really call the flight attendant 'waitress'?

We landed smoothly, taxied to the terminal and stopped. The usual lights and bells on board the plane kept everyone at bay. I stood in the aisle and pulled my valise down from above the guy in front of me who I noticed for the first time. It hit him in the head, accidentally, and messed up his hair. He looked quite agitated, but weighed no more than one hundred and forty pounds. I wasn't too concerned, but I apologized properly.

"Excuse me. I'm very sorry about that." We made eye contact briefly. He said nothing and proceeded into the aisle in front of me. He appeared vindicated. At the time, I had no idea that he was following me. We all gaggled our way out of the plane. That one flight attendant didn't look at me when I walked by. I was going to ask her what a guy had to do to get a cheeseburger and fries, but decided against it. She was wound pretty tight and someday would likely pop.

Baggage in hand, I found my way to the airport exit and a payphone. It was already Thursday morning! I called the valet parking service. It would only be a matter of minutes before my Chevy Lumina, driven by a cheerful valet parking employee, would arrive. No need to wait for a US Park shuttle. Besides, my credibility with them was still on the bottom. No shuttles for Frank Drachman. Nothing but the best! I walked outside and looked into the oncoming traffic.

There was the Lumina already, driven by a man older and more complicated looking than I would have expected. But he drove like, side-swiping another US park shuttle. I was impressed by his aggressive driving, and was nearly run over when he wheeled the car towards my bright-eyed waves. He stopped, got out and addressed me.

"Hello, Mr. Drachman." He walked around the back of the car and opened the trunk, then closed it when he realized I had only the valise and Franklin planner.

"How are you doing today?" I asked.

"Fine, sir. That's it for the luggage then?"

Then what? I wondered. "Yes, just the valise." Beth got it for me last Christmas. I wanted to think about her more but the valet was talking.

"Would you like to drive, Mr. Drachman?" he asked.

"Sure." We got into the car and I instinctively buckled my seat belt. He didn't. I pulled into traffic and cut off a US Park shuttle to merge. The key to offensive driving is to always give the other guy a chance to stop. He will, especially if it's a shuttle filled with passengers. My theory held true.

"So, from where are you returning?" he inquired, making light conversation in the hope of landing a larger trip.

Up close, I could see the deep wrinkles and pockmarks on his face. He had the look of a character actor in a gangster movie, not a valet driver.

"I was in Phoenix, on business. Didn't even get the chance to play golf."

"Pretty hot out there?"

"Sure was. Not much humidity though. Michigan in late July is worse." He didn't respond.

I worked my way slowly through traffic, passing the last terminal on the right before merging left, back towards the valet stop. Metro Airport was beginning to look modern. A brand-new steel-blue parking structure was going up right in the middle of everything.

Meanwhile, I felt around in my pocket, fumbling through the seat belt across my lap, for a couple of dollars. Only had a five. He'd get a good tip. I pulled it out and stuffed it into my shirt pocket. I slowed down to make the turn towards the valet stop. I looked over and saw four City of Romulus police cars – lights flashing – crammed into the parking lot there. Then the valet unzipped his jacket, which I suddenly noticed did not fit him right, and exposed a pistol. He took it in his left hand.

"Don't go back in," he commanded

Question marks flew from my head like popcorn from an uncovered pan. What in the world was happening? I had been carjacked! Kidnapped?

"If you are a police officer, I want you to know that I was going to go directly to the Dearborn Police Station."

"Get on I-94 west."

"What is going on?"

"Drive asshole, don't talk."

He was not a police officer, but he did have a gun. I decided to comply with his request and merged into the traffic on I-94 west.

"Where are we going?"

"Take this to I-275."

"North or south?"

"North, asshole."

What was his problem?

"Why asshole?" I inquired.

"What did you say, fucker?"

This was turning into a vintage male-to-male conversation.

"No, no, ah… not why asshole as in why comma asshole are we going north, but, ah, why are you calling me asshole so much?"

He regarded my words and paused. "Habit. I've got a lot of bad ones," he told me.

I drove on. About five seconds later, he smacked me hard on the right cheekbone with the butt of his pistol. It slightly dazed me.

"Why did you do that?"

"Just shut up and drive."

In the rear-view mirror, I saw blood trickle down my cheek. Between a hangover and this assault, my head hurt very, very much. It felt like Keith Moon was playing a one-man concert inside my skull. I felt angry and quiet. I felt blood pumping to my extremities. There was much tension and I was caring less about consequences. For twelve years I had worked hard and tried to do the right thing. Now, accused of murder, getting a divorce, my business just starting to take off, held at gunpoint in my own car, I was approaching a limit. What was the point to life? Was grandma right? If that son of a bitch hit me again, I would snap and do something drastic. The I-275 exit was approaching.

"Go north," he told me.

"Then what?"

Ten quiet minutes passed and the I-696 exits (east or west) approached.

"Take I-696 east," he said.

I was surprised he answered. A few more minutes passed. Traffic was scarce, and the sun was rising. I figured that he was going to take me to, say, downtown Pontiac, or maybe to Lake St. Clair, and shoot me dead. Why? I had absolutely no idea. But isn't that the key? Dealing with situations that we have little or no understanding of? Why did I stop loving Beth? I don't know, but I still have to deal with the results. These considerations gave me an idea: set it up so you know what will happen. Being an automotive test engineer had its advantages.

"Where is your computer? Why don't you travel with your computer?" he asked.

"What computer?"

"You know what computer, smart-ass."

"What are you talking about?" I asked.

"Do I have to fucking shoot you to get you to stop asking so many goddamned questions? Where is the laptop you bought at Arthur Bennington's estate sale?" He cocked the pistol.

"That computer is in my apartment."

"Good. Thank you."

"I live in Troy." I lied. I didn't think this was a case of random violence, and I was driving at a high rate of speed. Mr. carjacker would not kill the driver. I concluded that I need to find out what he knew about me.

"You live in Novi, asshole."

Okay, so he knew where I lived. He tried to hit me again, but I threw my head back and over his pistol butt came solidly down on my collar bone. This was extremely painful.

"What the hell are you doing? What is the point?" I said angrily. "I'm already bleeding, trying to drive."

"Don't lie to me or try to bullshit me. It won't work."

I knew that given the chance; he would have violated Kant's golden rule: I was a means to his end. It was more true than he would ever know. My computer was his end; that, and a sudden stop. We continued to drive eastward on the interstate. The exit for Coolidge Road was still a couple of miles away, and the tall, vertically ridged concrete walls that bordered the expressway on both sides looked as strong as the Great Wall of China.

The air bag system in my Lumina was controlled by an electronic module as reliable as the ones used to launch nuclear missiles and space shuttles. Most people don't know this, but I wear a seat belt. I was convinced that he had murdered before and was planning to kill me, too. Not today. Opportunities come and opportunities go. My eye was starting to swell. I was humiliated, powerless. The hell with him. We drove on.

"What exit do I get off?"

"I-75."

"North or south?"

"North, asshole."

The exit for Coolidge Road was still a mile (1.6 km) away. I felt my pulse racing like an out-of-control house fire. Sweating, I abruptly realized that I was still alive and did not want to die!

The distance between the left lane on eastbound I-696 and the concrete wall was about seventy-five feet, not quite enough to turn the vehicle perpendicular to the wall at sixty miles per hour. In case you are wondering, automobiles are designed to best protect the driver and passenger in a direct head-on collision, so long as they are wearing their seat belts. Working as a test engineer in the auto business pays off!

About a quarter mile before the Coolidge exit, near an entrance ramp onto I-696 from the service drive, the expressway curved gradually to the left. Since

I was going to make a sharp right-hand turn, it gave me a little more road to work with. The decision was made. I checked the rear-view mirror- no police, no traffic. In front of me was the beautiful orange sunrise.

I looked over at him, then at the gun. I simultaneously grabbed the barrel of the pistol with my right hand, pointing it upward, and turned the steering wheel with my sore left hand gradually more and more to the right, directly at the great wall. It was important not to turn the wheel too fast, so that the car did not fish out of control. The radial tires held, and the son of a bitch sitting next to me looked completely aghast. The gun fired and I felt heat on my right palm. But then I sat back in my chair, smiled, and held on tightly to the steering wheel and the barrel. The wall approached very rapidly, as in a fast-forwarded crash safety video. I pulled my feet back away from the pedals.

My Lumina, fully insured, ceased being an automobile – it transformed into a loud, crunching mass of steel and broken glass and seats. It was excruciatingly loud. We crashed head-on into the calm wall. I thought I heard the air bag explode, then felt a violent pull from the shoulder harness, which held me tight to the seat. Like a camera flash, it was over. We had gone from sixty miles per hour to zero miles per hour in about a tenth of a second.

There was white powder from the air bag on my clothes, and I had pissed my pants. I looked over at him. He was not moving and his legs were bent in funny ways. Blood seeped from his eyes and nose. The passenger-side air bag had deployed as expected, and snapped his neck. His legs and torso had slammed into the dashboard and floorboard. It looked like his left femur had snapped clean and tore through his flesh and pants. At least he won't chase me. My legs were not broken. I unbuckled the seat belt and climbed out through the shattered driver's door window opening. It was a tight fit. Everything seemed to be fine except for my right hand. I was still clutching the barrel of his pistol.

A few cars had stopped and people cautiously approached me.

"Are you alright?" said someone. "I've called an ambulance."

"He's got a gun!" screamed another.

"I think so," I answered. Slowly, things cleared up. I had been fortunate. Then I heard sirens and concluded that it was the Dearborn Police Department on their way to railroad me. A short distance away was the entrance ramp onto I-696. I made for it in a slow jog. The gun kept everyone at a distance.

"Where are you going?" another person asked.

"I have a business to run." Gradually, I began to move faster and the voices trailed off, canceled by road and city noise. I reached the entrance ramp, slowed to a walk, then proceeded up against traffic.

CHAPTER THREE

On a typical day, peers believe peers. This explains why some can fool others.

Gaston Haddock

Five or six cars drove past me as I trudged up the entrance ramp. It felt strange being the object of such queer interest again, like when Beth and I announced to all involved that we were getting a separation to be followed soon by a divorce. Everybody I had once known with her had developed this aura of *'What in the hell really happened with them?'* I never told, but maybe Beth did. She ended up with more friends. The people driving on the ramp probably would have liked her better too. They looked at me for as long as possible, all craning their necks. I certainly looked and felt horrible. Tired, hung-over, messy, and unshaven. And, of course, the dead man's pistol now tucked into my belt.

Back on I-696, police cars and fire trucks roared in the distance, racing for the crash site. I felt the urge to hurry, began to jog again, and soon reached the top of the entrance ramp where I saw a police car approaching, lights flashing, on the service drive.

I did not know what to do, so I instinctively ran across the service drive, to the south side, and hid behind a telephone pole. The squad car raced by and descended on the freeway entrance ramp where two minutes earlier I had been the main attraction! I waited about five minutes more behind the wooden telephone pole, then headed east toward Coolidge Road. There, I could find a payphone and call somebody for trusted help. But who?

The Dearborn Police were probably watching Cindy Salome very closely. Maybe it was best to simply turn myself in. But what about Arthur Bennington and his estate sale? I needed more information! And what about my computer?

I had no plans to kill anyone else that day, not even accidentally. So, as I walked along the service drive toward Coolidge Road, I removed the bullets from the pistol. There were five left. I put them in my pants' pocket. I was wearing a pair of olive green Tommy Hilfiger's, from Hudson's. It was the first time all day that I had noticed what clothes I was wearing. The creases down the front center of the pant legs were vague, almost gone, as if they were hung incorrectly on a wooden hanger. They were out of form. And my mind was completely caught up with being a fugitive, suspected of murder.

Then I checked my shirt pocket for that five-dollar bill, but it was gone. Must have flown out at the great wall. The valet got his tip. I had no other money, no credit cards, no identification, which wasn't all bad considering I was a fugitive, and no wallet. Where did it go? My future was not looking bright: no need for sunglasses. I walked on.

Soon I came upon a stop sign on the service drive. Over my left shoulder, I saw a brand new Jeep Cherokee slow down, stop, and wait for the I-696 exit-to-Coolidge traffic. In a rapid motion, I twisted and pulled the gun out of my pants, walked to the front of the vehicle, and pointed it at the driver, who could have easily run me down but didn't. He was young, big man with his elbow on the window opening.

He appeared quite shocked when he saw the gun, and then looked over his bulky right shoulder at a child strapped into a safety seat in the rear. "Don't shoot," he screamed.

"I need a ride somewhere, that's all," I told him firmly.

He reached back to get his child. A little girl. "Take the car! Just don't shoot!" He was frenzied.

"No," I said. "Stay in the car. I do not want to hurt anyone. You've got to drive me." I felt like a piece of dog shit for pointing a gun at this young father, even though I knew he was in no danger.

Then he started to look angry.

I held the gun on him as I moved left, to the passenger's side door. He was no gambler and did not drive away. If he had been alone, he would have run me down. "I'm going to get into the Jeep," I told him.

"If anything happens to my daughter, I'll rip your nuts off!" He was an articulate speaker.

I believed him, and came very close to handing him the gun and giving up. What in the hell was I doing?

His baby daughter was crying. It frightened her to see her daddy so angry.

"I have no plans or desire to hurt you," I assured them.

"Then what do you want?" he asked. I noticed that his vehicle had air bags, and that his daughter was strapped into a certified child safety seat.

I buckled the seat belt. "Take me to Twelve Oaks Mall, The Hudson's. That's all I need," I stated.

He then spoke gently to his little daughter, "It's okay, Bonnie. Daddy is just going to give this man a ride to work." She was about three years old and believed him wholeheartedly and stopped crying. That was fine with her. The young father rubbed her hair on top and then the back of her tiny head tenderly with his big right hand. "Then you are going to school."

"Okay, daddy," she replied contentedly.

I felt nauseous and almost passed out. Not from their warmth, but from everything. The stress or guilt, I don't know. How dare I interrupt this man's morning drive to daycare with his daughter. How could I be wanted for the murder of Ian Hatley? There was just no way to prove it, right?

"I am sorry to put you through this. I'm in the middle of something that I don't quite understand. All I need is a ride. Nothing more." I attempted to put him at ease. Of course, without the gun I was no match for him. He could have beaten the shit out of me. I could change my name to Ian. He was younger and bigger and more passionate. He was no test engineer, probably something more well-rounded.

Before I knew it, my hostage had pulled onto the next traffic overpass, to drive west on I-696. Rush hour was in full swing. Between incompetent drivers and this young man's patient maneuvering, we did not arrive at Twelve Oaks Mall for about forty-five minutes. He and I said nothing, and Bonnie sang a Barney song. He got off the freeway at the mall exit and wheeled into the empty parking lot by Hudson's, where I then noticed he had a Motorola cell phone. I still had no money.

"I need to take the phone," I told him. He picked it up and scratched at a label that was Scotch taped to the battery pack.

"You can have the damn phone, but I don't want you to know where I live." Did he believe that I was a desperate person who wanted to hurt him or his child? Something in the tone of his voice told me that he might.

"Fine," I replied, and took the phone from him.

"Well, this is where you said you wanted to go."

"Right. Thanks." I got out. It was a relief to know he no longer felt in danger. The tires on his Grand Cherokee squealed away. My apartment was only a quarter of a mile away from Twelve Oaks Mall. Using his cell phone, I dialed my home number and it rang and rang. What did I expect? I hit the 'END' button and stuffed the antenna back into the phone. I noticed on the battery pack the label that the young man had tried to remove. It read: 'Property of Brook

Tabe'. The last part of his last name was torn away. Brook Tabe would have a story to tell his wife.

So there I stood, in the middle of an empty parking lot, surrounded by retail stores packed into a mall named after trees that did not really exist. Across the parking lot, to the east, there was a drainage ditch and a chain-link fence. On the other side of the fence stood the apartment complex to which I had recently moved. I walked over and climbed the seven foot fence and dropped hard onto the other side, where, in the clearing by my building, I saw two police cars - one from Dearborn, one from Novi. Shit.

I almost turned myself in again, then Ian Hatley crossed my mind. And who carjacked me? The crash scene on I-696 would have been the time to say fuck it and give it all up. Turn up the Led Zeppelin and unbuckle the seat belt. Why didn't I just do that? But I had decided what I had decided and had to live with it! Consequently, there were two basic assumptions a logical person could make. First, Arthur Bennington was not simply a retired executive from General Motors who had mentored Burt Morgan, as I had been told by Burt himself. Why would anyone kill for Bennington's old laptop computer? Second, the Dearborn Police really thought I had murdered Ian Hatley. It was the latter point that troubled me the most.

By now though, that young father had reported me to the police. I too was a carjacker! If the cops at my apartment got the word to search the Twelve Oaks area, they would have to drive right back down the road I was now walking on. I needed to get the hell out of there and save myself.

There were several other things to do: call Burt Morgan, call Cindy Salome. No. Neither could truly help. Call my parents. No. We hadn't talked much, really, since I married Beth. I tried to convince them that she was right for me, but they were wrong in their own way. Somehow, things with them always ended up focused on my older brother Michael.

He died in the upper peninsula. Sorry if I'm being repetitive, but like I said, he keeps coming up. We were driving back to Michigan Tech for my senior year and his sophomore year. Mike was older than me, but after high school he worked and decided four years later to get educated. No, I could certainly not call my parents. I had developed a skill for crashing cars and coming out unharmed. But I still had no one to call. The police at my apartment went nowhere.

As I turned back towards the fence and mall, I just could not get it out of my head how Mike and me and dad would play catch in a triangle when he got home from work, and how my mother would happily call us all for dinner from the front porch. It was wonderful, and it was over. I climbed the fence again.

On the other side, I sat down on a parking block and realized that everything that was ever important to me was just gone. No getting it back. There seemed no other way. Thank God, because he did what he could. But then, that morning, I had nothing else to draw on. Relief was the short-term goal - the only goal. It felt like my last finals week.

My mother's father gave me money and encouragement for college, and then he paid for my entire final term at Tech because his favorite grandson Michael died too soon. Grandpa needed to do something. He was a plumber from Iowa who believed school was the best thing. He made it through sixth grade and would often say, "Your shit is my bread and butter." When I was a boy and he said that, I always imagined a shit sandwich. Even now I dislike Nutella.

He told me at Mike's funeral that I only had to reimburse him for tuition and room and board if I graduated in the top quarter of my class at Michigan Tech. Because, he maintained, 'For Christ's sake, Frank, if you can't be in the top quarter of a class at a second rate engineering school in northern Michigan, I don't want to burden you further with repayment. That place is no MIT. Things will be tough enough. And besides, Mike could have.'

I graduated twenty-sixth out of three hundred and fifty-five electrical engineers, but gramps died before I could pay him back. Two months after commencement, another fucking funeral. He must have updated his will frequently though, because in it he said how proud and happy he was that Frank would repay St. Vincent DePaul all the money he had given him for school. After the reading of the will, my mother said, "Don't worry about that." Growing up Catholic was very complex - there were subplots everywhere. I loved my grandpa and missed my brother, and I wanted to talk to my dad. Damn.

Twelve Oaks Mall was just opening and I needed several things. I repackaged the unloaded, impressive-looking pistol and the stolen cell phone in my pants and untucked my shirt so it would cover them. I went into Hudson's.

I shopped quickly. Underwear, black Tommy Hilfiger pants, black turtleneck, and black socks. Dress the part (spy). With the clothes draped over my arm and a vacant cash register, the moment of truth arrived. It was easy. I simply walked right out, as though they had refused to give me a refund. Fine! How dare they! Indignation is a fine weapon. I was becoming good at these things, and thought about Ron LeFlore before he joined the Tigers. Prior to pilfering bases, he stole from countless stores. Do what you're good at, because if you don't, someone else will.

Outside Hudson's, a new wardrobe in hand, the air was warm; and across Novi Road, west of Twelve Oaks Mall, there were many stores blossoming. K-Mart, F&M, Arbor Drugs, Kerby's Coney Island, and on and on. Most of them sold all the same shit, hot dogs excluded. But I needed a razor and some deodorant. A shower too. How? With what money? I needed help. Cindy Salome. There she was again.

I had her work number memorized, among other things. Would I call on this pretty, vivacious woman who said she loved me and said Beth was foolish, and who did not know the whole story and who I had not even called back? Yes, I would. Besides, we had always eaten at good restaurants and there was nobody else to call.

Cindy and I first slept together the night we met at Friday's at Fairlane to discuss the overall vision of the AAMA subcommittee, two days after the first meeting, and five days before the second meeting. This must have been three months ago. At the second meeting, GM (me) and Ford (Cindy) were suddenly on the same page for several of the issues. Of course, Burt Morgan needed a bit of convincing, but I was up to the task. Burt was in good hands. Cindy had more than one way with me. Now, though, things were complicated.

If Brook Tabe-whatever was what he seemed, his cell phone theft would certainly be reported, leaving me soon with no way to communicate. I dialed Cindy's work number, hit the 'SEND' button, and it rang three times.

"Good morning, Cindy Salome, body electrical," she answered.

I paused there in the parking lot, thinking, holding the Motorola cell phone close to my left ear, and imagined her sitting at her desk, working diligently.

As near as I could figure, she must have been assigned to the AAMA subcommittee on electromagnetic compatibility under duress, as any normal person would have felt. Her goal was to put into place the ideals of some underpaid manager want-to-be. overpaid executive engineer. It was similar to my agreement with Burt Morgan.

The reason GM and Ford wanted something different here was grounded in the oldest root cause - resistance to change. Or, perhaps, reluctance to spend a lot of money on equipment for tests that gave very little new helpful data? Or was it politics?

"Hello, is anyone there?"

"Cindy, it's Frank."

"Frank!" Neither of us listened well.

"I got your message, Cindy. Thanks for trying to let me know. I'm in a really tight spot."

"The police call me almost every day, and that Officer Munday is a fucking bitch. I don't think she likes you very much." She whispered the swear words.

"Easy with the good news, Cindy. What does she ask about?"

"What do you think?" She was angry at me.

"What did you tell her?"

"What do you think I told her?" Whew. Question with a question. Cindy sounded like Beth when Beth and I met at the lawyer's office to discuss the divorce last week (I don't recall the day).

At that time, I asked Beth if we could split what was left when the house was finally sold. My lawyer told me before the meeting that it could surely never hurt to ask, especially if she still loved me or felt guilty. Knowledge of somebody's moral guilt could be quite useful. But Beth didn't feel guilty and she had a good lawyer - Seth Fein was his name. Beth replied, "What do you think?"

My settlement with Beth would probably cost me something more than what I took into the debacle, and I still had to somehow squeeze it out of Forward Research and Test. Beth was very angry, and chided and challenged me about it.

Ben David said, "Frank, don't engage in this argument." I snapped back to the present.

"Okay, look, Cindy, I am really sorry to involve you now in this. Do you want me to hang up and forget about you?" I guessed that she didn't.

"Frank, did you do it?"

"What do you think?"

"I need to hear you say it."

"Say what, Cindy? I need some goddamned help! Can you help me?"

"Oh, Frank. What are you... what do you want me to do?"

She hung up, sobbing.

Time was running out. Soon, the cell phone would be locked or the battery would die, or some fucking thing. And I still had no money and no place to turn.

It would be very stupid to turn myself in. Ben David Fisher would know what to do, so I dialed his office number. Most lawyers give you the number for the main receptionist at their firm. Ben told me that he did this, except with divorce cases.

Seemed that when clients called, they wanted to immediately talk to the person who was responsible for making everything all right. Ben was my clergy. Two rings and he answered.

"Hello, Brook. How's little Bonnie doing?" I was numb.

Why did he say Brook?

"Brook who?" I replied.

"Is this not Brook Taberman?"

"No, it's Frank Drachman."

"Frank Drachman?"

"Yes, Frank Drachman. Who is Brook Taberman?"

"Unless there's something wrong with my beta copy cell phone caller ID, you're calling from Brook Taberman's cell phone." Then it hit me: Brook Tabe... and his daughter Bonnie!

"How do you know Brook Taberman?" I demanded.

"He's an intern at my firm."

"You've got to be kidding." I told him. My last bastion of legal hope, my lawyer, Ben David Fisher, worked with the younger man that I carjacked earlier this morning!

"No, Frank, I'm quite serious. What is going on?"

"Ben", I began, "there's not enough time to explain. I've got to go."

"Frank, talk to me..."

His voice trailed off as my arm dropped to my side. Then I pressed the 'END' button.

Since cellular phones are very easy to monitor, with their signals flying all around, it made sense that a lawyer would want to know who was calling before answering. Drug dealers, intensely employable here in the Detroit area, were always on the lookout for respected legal representation. Ben David Fisher's firm had the absolute latest technology, with all employees preprogrammed for rapid identification. Someone there must have read John Grisham.

I had to call Cindy, or give up. Again, Cindy's familiar number.

"Cindy Salome, body electrical."

"Cindy, it's me again. Don't hang up, please. There are two things I have to tell you."

"I can't believe this mess," she cried quietly. It amazed me how she could immediately feel.

"Cindy, I love you." Silence. Then, "Oh, Frank, I love you too. Why now? Why not a month ago?" She was tough.

"I don't know, Cindy. But I need some help." I was a real shit.

"To do what? If you didn't do it then just turn yourself in. You'll be okay if you're innocent." Cindy thought O.J. was innocent; it was part of her charm. She also thought he was very attractive.

"It's not that simple anymore."

"What do you mean?"

"I need help. Can you meet me?"

"I don't know." She replied. Then after a short pause, "Okay, where?"

"Remember the manager's office at my apartment complex?"

"Yes."

"Tonight, ten o'clock. I'll come from around the back of the office as soon as you pull in. Come alone."

"All right."

She came through for me and it felt nice. "Thanks more than you know. See you tonight."

"Goodbye, Frank."

"Oh Cindy," I remembered, "I need money, cash, as much as you can spare!" The cell phone went dead. Did she hear me?

There were twelve hours to kill. Perhaps it was the time to try to answer some questions. Perhaps not. I was so hungry that decisions were impossible. I folded the Motorola phone up into almost nothing and put it into my left pants' pocket.

Since stealing the spy clothes from Hudson's, I did not venture too far, maybe thirty feet from the door, and was making phone calls to friends and accomplices on a stolen phone with the hope that they would further assist me, an accused felon. Standing there, unshaven and looking cruddy, I noticed that the parking lot was getting full and Hudson's patrons avoided me. It was time to get a move on.

The K-Mart across Novi Road was my salvation. I would fit in perfectly at the cafeteria, quietly enjoying a half-eaten Hoagie and frozen Coke. Man was I hungry. I meandered through the cars in the huge Hudson's parking lot. It felt like a flat anthill. Everywhere I looked: people and cars! But I continued, crossing Novi Road with clothes in hand, and ten minutes later arrived at the entrance to K-Mart and went in.

Plundering around near the checkout lines, looking irritated with a swollen cheek, carrying unbagged clothes, I drew no attention. They had seen my type many times. In the rear of the building was the cafeteria, and I headed there directly. Broke and hungry, leftovers were my only option.

Upon entering the dining area, I spotted a partially eaten ham submarine sandwich surrounded by a pile of broken potato chips at an unoccupied booth. This combination was suddenly my personal favorite, so I walked by, picked up the sub, hid it under the spy clothes, then proceeded to sit down at a nearby clean, empty booth. There, I began to look intently for no one. Several minutes passed. The K-Mart brunch crowd turned over. I took the sandwich out and ate it in four bites. Such leftovers reminded me of college, but damn they were satisfying.

My talent for deception did not bother me; rather, it was exhilarating. It felt wonderful to not have to be Frank W. Drachman! But after two very long days, I was getting tired. The cheekbone hurt too. Cindy Salome would not be there to help for several more hours. And then what? Suddenly the K-Mart cafeteria was no comfort. My mind was drowning. I had to get out. Past several blue light specials I marched, clinging to the change of stolen clothes from Hudson's. Just outside the entrance, I stood facing the parking lot. The air was warming and others' pursuits of rubble were in full swing.

I turned left and walked to the end of the building and turned left again and walked to the back of the building and turned left one more time. I found myself alone and very tired, like at Mike's funeral. Then I saw several big blue dumpsters lined up against the back of the building like pawns on a chessboard and was drawn to them. Up close, they all smelled rotten and moldy. But there was nobody around to see me climb into the nearest one. I had eaten and needed to sleep. Food and rest.

CHAPTER FOUR

Those dark hours will either break you or not. And there will be other effects which are not so clear.

Cameron Barnes

It was getting dark when I awoke, lying in trash. What time was it? What day was it? Thursday. It was Thursday. Would Cindy show? Would Andy answer? Plausible denial? There was no way to know. Should I call Burt Morgan? What would he think? I thought of Burt as an educated version of my father, or grandfather, or something. Not that education made you a better person. No, it did nothing, deep down, of the kind, but it did peel away and discard the most hampering layers. Thanks to education, I landed my first engineering job twelve years ago (right after I graduated) with the United States government, designing the electrical system of M1 Abrams tanks at the Warren Tank Arsenal. I was so happy to get this job that out of appreciation I bought Will and Ariel Durant's eleven volume *History of Civilization* for my grandpa. Without his help, I would not have had that opportunity. I also wanted to help him understand how the world had always worked; that Michael's death five months earlier was reasonably natural in the overall, big picture, scheme of things, but it did no good that I could see. Gramps died naturally (heart attack in his sleep) a month after I gave him the books. So I reclaimed them and gave them to my dad. No word from him yet. Twelve years is a long time to wait, but every one of those volumes is like a James Michener novel.

Now, with Beth and the others gone, Burt Morgan was all I had. Or was he? Burt had managed to survive and prosper in the jungle of General Motors. He was what I wanted to be. Or was he? People don't know how difficult that road is. But I doubt if I will achieve what he had achieved. Just ask Beth. Very likely, my corporate journey to the top was over. After all, I had just napped in a dumpster! I tried his number but the phone battery died before the first ring. I checked my watch - it was a quarter to ten I changed into the rumpled spy clothes that had served as my pillow for the past several hours, buckled my belt, and climber out of the dumpster, leaving the phone, gun, and bullets behind Cindy Salome would soon be waiting for me in front of the manager's office. It was time to move.

While jogging back towards Twelve Oaks Mall and my apartment complex, I became excited about the chase I was in. There was nothing more to be anxious about; I was doing everything I could, considering. This was living! I found my way over the fence and into the bushes near the manager's building.

Cindy arrived exactly on time. I waited behind an evergreen in front of the office for only five minutes and was overjoyed at her arrival. She drove a Mercury Mystique. It was turning into a rough year for Ford, and people in the industry who didn't know better were calling the Mystique the 'mistake'. It was well known that Ford's upper management decided that the best way for Ford to survive was to be the American Toyota - the highest quality automobile manufacturer in the world. But quality was in fact expensive, not free; Phil Crosby - God help his theory - was wrong.

Ford's latest cars were magnificent: the Mustang, Taurus, F-Series truck. Problem was that people couldn't afford them like they used to and often bought a Plymouth or Chevy instead. Sales were down.

I ran out from the bushes and pulled at the passenger's door handle. It was locked! Had I been set up? No. Cindy was nervous and forgot to unlock the door; after she saw me and did so, I climbed in smelling like the garbage of K-Mart.

"Cindy," I said, "thanks for coming. Let's go."

"Frank, you look awful. What happened to your cheek?"

"I can't go into that right now."

"I didn't mean—"

"I know. Don't worry about it. Thanks for getting me."

"Frank, I'm confused. What are you going to do?" Cindy had not stopped asking the difficult questions, the ones I avoided. She could be the right woman for me. Beth was too busy nagging and ragging about meaningless bullshit to ask such things. She was an unhappy soul, bent on showing the proper appearances. The capitalist's friend. Beth used a mirror to fix her make-up, nothing else. Toward the end, I got pissed off whenever she said anything.

"Right now, I don't know. Planning is a growth area for me. Did you bring the cash?" She drove slowly out of the apartment complex.

"Yes. Where do you want to go?" She asked.

"I'm sorry to bring you into this. There are some things I've got to find out and then I'll know the right thing to do. How much money did you bring?"

"I have eight hundred in cash." Then she pressed, "Why are you running around like this? I can't believe you would do that to somebody. Can't you take a lie detector test?"

"Look, Cindy, or should I say, Officer Salome? I am doing the best I can and your help is everything to me right now."

"Well, I still don't know why you won't tell me!" She was impatient.

"There's nothing to tell, yet."

"Fine!" she exclaimed. "I give up. Now where do you want to go?"

"To my old house," I replied calmly.

"Where Beth lives?"

"Yes. I need to get something."

"What could you possibly need from there?"

"It's too complicated to get into."

"Of course it is," she commented sarcastically.

"Do you remember how to get there?"

"Not exactly. I was only there once, you know."

"I know. Get on I-696 east to Lahser." She got on the expressway and drove to Lahser. "Then," I continued, "take Lahser—"

"I remember now," she said.

After that moment, with her sweet, solemn voice and smell filling the car, my life felt frozen in disbelief. I was getting a divorce. I was wanted for murder.

"Can I have the eight hundred dollars?"

"Sure." She took a packet of twenty dollar bills wrapped in a rubber band from her purse and handed it to me.

"Thanks. I will pay you back." But it was time to get Cindy out of this mess. I did not want her to get into any more trouble than was already possible. Her loyalty and money were priceless. And that question kept coming from her, almost supernaturally: What was I doing?

Two things were operating. First, if the dead carjacker from the airport wanted the computer I had bought from Arthur Bennington's estate sale, then he, or whomever he worked for, could have it. Whatever they were after was probably hidden on some sector of the hard drive. That's just how these things worked, I had recently concluded. But the first thing I replaced on that machine, the next day in fact, was the hard drive. The original drive was still at my old house in the basement electronics junk box, which I forgot to take when I moved out.

The second thing involved my dear friend, Andy Brooks. The head-on car crash that killed my brother Mike, nearly killed Andy too. He was driving the other car, alone. The accident occurred on a stretch of Highway 28 about twenty miles east of Marquette, the upper peninsula's largest city. At the time, Andy worked as a civilian employee at the now closed KI Sawyer Air Force Base near Marquette. He was on his way home, heading east. Mike and I were going west, as young men should, and I lost control of the car. Let me describe how.

A gust of wind from Lake Superior pushed the 1972 Buick LeSabre I was driving across the center line of the icy road. Mike sat in the passenger's seat next to me. There were six or seven empty beer cans at his feet. We had both drank a few. When I tried to gently turn right to ease back across to the right side of the road, the car fishtailed and I had to cut the wheel left to keep from spinning. Goddamn bias ply tires. By then it was too late. We were skating on the wrong side of the road at sixty-five miles per hour. Andy was about two hundred feet away, according to the police report, before he realized I was driving directly at him. There was nothing either of us could have done to avoid it, according to the police report. And so we collided head-on. My seat belt held, Mike's didn't, Andy's did.

Andy was driving a Dodge K-car and it bounced off the two and a half ton Buick like a tennis ball. I remember seeing Andy's eyes get really big just before impact. The Dodge sort of half slid and half flew into the ditch along the road to my right and flipped over. There were no explosions; a rarity, according to the police report, for an accident involving such high speeds and cold, dry air. The Buick kept going straight on the road for another hundred or so feet, but after it was about six feet shorter and had my brother's body on the hood. Apparently, his seat belt held for a split second after impact and then was pulled right out from the bolts. It was enough to keep him from flying rapidly through the windshield over the top of Andy's K-car. It looked like a couple of longshoremen had swung him like a sack of bloody potatoes onto the Buick's hood from the top of the car. I never looked at his dead face at the accident scene. I couldn't look at him dead like that, but I knew he was dead.

I waited awhile – I have no idea how long – and fought my way out the windshield opening and staggered with two fractured ankles to Andy's car. Thin, weak ankles were a legacy in my family. It was very dark and very cold that night. I heard Andy moaning, and that's all I remember. I don't think I could have pulled him from the car, but according to the police report, I did. So for the past twelve years, Andy has thought that I saved his life. He would do anything for me. He turned into my connection to Mike, and I would do anything for him.

After the accident, we kept in touch, exchanging letter maybe once a month discussing our medical rehabilitation, I healed quickly physically. The doctors said my body had recovered very well. For

Mike's funeral I needed a wheelchair, but I was back on my feet (with crutches) in two weeks and back to college (with crutches) in three. My plumber grandpa told me, "Mike is gone now, so get on with it." His shit was not my bread and butter. My parents said little. I complied and was able to catch up and finish all degree requirements; graduation was not delayed. What would be the point to that?

For two men writing letters, Andy and I grew to be close friends. This went on for several years and, gradually, more time passed between letters. Then, in 1992, the airbase where he worked was deemed unnecessary by the Pentagon. More money was needed for people who didn't work. I offered him a job at Forward Research and Test and he accepted. We have worked together for over three years and have come to know each other's daily ups and downs. When he saw my broken nose two months ago, he wanted to know who did it. I assured him that I could look out for myself but told him about Ian Hatley anyway.

Andy was a former marine who owed me his life. He knew about avenging these things. That was my problem. I had not been able to contact Andy to see if he knew something about Ian Hatley. And I certainly couldn't tell Cindy all this. The most important thing right now was to get my hands on that discarded hard drive.

I flashed through these thoughts and then noticed we had arrived at the Thirteen Mile Road and Laser area of Southfield. Many homes and roads on irregularly placed lots connected by unlit, winding side streets. Cindy turned mechanically right onto Highland, my old street. If she had been talking to me, I had not heard her for at least ten minutes.

Then she asked, "Where do you want to get out?"

"Right here," I replied. 'Here' was about a quarter mile from the house.

"Then what?"

"Nothing more, Cindy. You have helped me more than I could have ever expected, and I can't involve you anymore. I'm in big, deep shit."

"I would do more if you asked."

"You have done more than enough for now. You have no idea how much I appreciate this."

"Don't spend that money all in one place," she grinned sadly.

"Thank you." I leaned over and kissed her half on the mouth and half on the cheek and smelled her shiny dark hair.

"I love you."

"Me too." I can't remember who said what first, but it didn't matter.

"I will get in touch with you when I can."

"Promise?"

"Promise." I got out thinking about it, and closed the door. She didn't wait around long and drove off into the darkness. Walking behind her disappearing car, I wondered why I hadn't married her instead of Beth. Probably because you didn't know her, dumb shit. Then I snapped out of it and thought about breaking and entering my old house - child's play compared to murder.

All the houses in the old subdivision looked the same in the darkness. You couldn't see any of them. A few dogs barked at my smell as I walked. A few minutes later I saw from a distance that no lights were on at Beth's house – she wasn't home yet. And, since she was going to keep the place, I figured at that moment it was time for me to get used to the idea.

The plan was to sneak in, get the hard drive, sneak out. Very complicated. The screen in the window above the kitchen sink was easy to remove from the outside, and we had always left that window unlocked. I hoped that she hadn't changed in that regard. The kitchen was located toward the rear of the house, so I approached and ran quickly around to the back of the house.

A few weeks before Ian Hatley broke my nose, Beth and I returned shit-faced from a party at her squash club, the Tap and Roll Racquet Club, and decided to take a walk. We had a nice walk and laid the keys on the kitchen table before leaving, locking ourselves out. That night we discovered an alternative route inside our home without breaking a window. As prototype drunks, we were quite creative. And the kitchen window was on our side too. I hoisted Beth onto my shoulders, knowing all the While that we had good medical coverage. We were not far from a separated shoulder or stitches, but everything went as hoped. She managed to work the storm screen out from the window frame with only minor damage and we had not locked the window on the inside. Our marriage was fractured, buckling and a shit hole, but the window opened and I lowered Beth to the ground like a camel. She lifted her long left leg over my head and hopped off. She was wearing tight blue jeans, well. I stood up, jumped into the opening, and pulled myself halfway through, hand-walking over the sink. Beth laughed and was pinching my butt, giggling, saying, "What are you gonna do about it?" She did have a wonderful laugh. I fell onto the eggshell linoleum kitchen floor, plotting.

Back to being a fugitive. I checked the window, and it was open and the house was empty. Where was she? I still wondered about her, among others. Who was I to ask? Adrenaline helped me climb quickly through the window. I slid over the sink and flopped onto the floor and stood up immediately, like a below average figure skater who did not intend to fall.

The basement was connected to the rest of the house by stairs, which started next to the kitchen to my left as I faced away from the sink. I went down. It was very sad. Nothing was disturbed. Beth probably didn't come down here except to do laundry. It was apparent that she had not yet dealt with my leaving. She was surely depressed and alone, consistent with her unfinished basement: one big room containing a washer and dryer and several boxes on wooden shelves. Dark, dank, and empty. Glum. A metaphor for divorce. God help her.

The box I wanted was still there, marked electrical crap in my hand. It was a box full of things I'd saved for no apparent reason. There was even an eight-track tape player! Every time! hear 'Seasons of

Wither' by Aerosmith, I anticipate that track change – it really adds to the song. They should incorporate it into CDs – it would sell. The first time I heard it I was almost seventeen; now, I'm almost thirty-five. Denial was very powerful, just like 'Get Your Wings'. The hard drive was there too, and I picked it out and replaced the box on its bottom shelf. It was time to go. Poor Beth. My throat and hands hurt. I remembered when I loved her, then I heard the front door open upstairs. Shit! Damn! Hell! Actually, I did not care and there was no need to cuss. There was no reason to be afraid of my wife, except that she was not alone.

She was with a man I knew. So soon? Was it his laugh, or movement? What signs had I missed? The storm door slapped shut, then one of them pushed close the big, wooden door. Their voices were happy and muffled, but I recognized his voice from somewhere. It was Ed Finninen! Ed Finninen? I was paralyzed. Ed was a straight shooter, a former ROTC student at Michigan Tech. He had married the daughter of a banker. Or was he divorced too? What next?!

There was still a phone in the laundry area. I heard the TV upstairs go on. I called information for a taxi service that operated in the area, dialed the number, and told them to pick me up at my old address on Highland in fifteen minutes. I could hear the duo upstairs and it was good to hear Beth laugh instead of bitch, even though I was hiding in her basement. As far as I remembered, she and Ed had met only once, at a Christmas party or something.

Wrong again? Might this help my divorce settlement? Probably not, considering my own activities.

From the bottom of the stairway, I saw no light diffracting through the kitchen from the family room. They were in the dark. I didn't want to imagine them together, but on the other hand, if they were distracted enough, pawing at each other, then perhaps I could sneak outside straight through the front door without being noticed. There are always opportunities in every situation and you just have to see them. I decided to climb the stairs and investigate what Ed Finninen and my wife were up to.

I proceeded to the kitchen and sat in front of the sink. At that location, the family room was to my right. Ahead, slightly to the left, was the hallway which led to the front door. The empty living room was to the right, opening into the hallway. There wasn't much time, maybe ten minutes, and the taxi would beep its horn out front.

Based on how things had gone the prior two days, there was just no way the taxi would be late. Not today. It would arrive dead nuts on time, if not earlier. If I wasn't out there, Ed, or maybe Beth, I don't know, would go out and ask what the taxi driver wanted. And the driver would tell Ed or Beth in angry broken English that a fare called for a pick-up at this address. No, there is no mistake, this is the address. An undetermined amount of time would then be required to explain to the driver that nobody needs a taxi, thanks. Then, Ed, or Beth, would come back inside and tell the other how strange it was, and the two of them would be acutely aware of their surroundings and detect me hiding in the fucking basement and I would be fucked, or caught, or both. My mind raced.

Then: "Ed, turn off the TV and take me."

I froze. WTF? Had Beth started reading D.H. Lawrence? She never used to talk like that to me. Take me?

Ed climbed off of her, still dressed, and walked to the TV and shut it off. They were both breathing heavily. I could see his dark silhouette through the doorway opening between the kitchen and family room and wanted to be gone. Beth was lying on her back on the love seat facing the TV; I could see only her feet dangling over the edge. Ed stood by the TV, dropped his trousers and slid down his briefs, while Beth worked off the bottom half of her wardrobe.

With the television now turned off, there was no way I could leave undetected. What could I do? Maybe I could create some kind of distraction that would last just long enough to keep Beth and Ed from noticing my escape. I went back downstairs to my electrical junk box. Fumbling quietly, I pulled out the universal TV-VCR programmable remote-control clicker and pressed some buttons. The red light lit; the batteries were still good! I bought it when I temporarily lost the original remote for the portable TV I kept in our, my, informal divorce agreement.

Then I turned on the laundry light and located the instruction manual in the junk box that had the programmable codes in it. I opened the booklet to the 'S' code page, found Sharp, and saw '446' as the code for 'most Sharp TVs'. Following the instructions was easy and I programmed the universal remote to control my old TV. It was touching.

I turned the light off and quietly trudged up to the top of the stairs holding the hard drive and remote control, and knelt on the third step from the landing there. I heard clear dialogue. They had made it to that point and it was awkward and Beth spoke up.

"Ed, wait. Let me get a condom," she breathed.

I peered around the corner.

He pulled back onto his knees and Beth swung her right leg in front of his face, sat, and then stood up. She walked with no pants briskly to the bathroom located by the kitchen and landing next to where the basement met. About six feet from where I was hiding.

The medicine cabinet opened and closed.

I thought about that American pilot shot down over Bosnia, how he never moved even when the enemy walked right next to him. My inspiration.

Beth passed back through the kitchen and cooperated with Ed. Soon, those unmistakable sounds emanated from my old family room.

Depending on their chemistry, one or both of them was due to attain in a matter of seconds. Maybe they would arrive together and not even notice one fugitive leaving through the front door. No such luck. Ed went first. As he started, I thought 'the hell with distractions' and floated undetected through the kitchen, as in a dream, with the old hard drive under my left arm and the remote control in my left hand. When I reached the hallway to the front door, Beth started. God help me if Ed didn't have enough left to keep them both occupied a few seconds more.

"Ed. Oh Ed. Oh, oh, oh…"

The door was unlocked and I pulled it open as they jointly bellowed in chorus and I wanted to be out of there and moved through the opening. Instead of finishing the exit, however, I stopped and pointed the remote control back into the house at the family room. I pressed the on/off button and saw the red light. The TV popped on loudly and I heard Beth say something other than "Oh Ed," and Ed spoke too, but I didn't make out the words. And then I closed the door quietly. Enough was enough.

Outside there were countless stars and a taxi pulled into the driveway of my ex-home. I tossed my remote into the bush and held onto the hard drive and climbed into the taxi, upset.

"Good evening, sir," the driver said. "Where do you want to go?"

"I'm not quite sure," I replied. "Just drive forty dollars worth, into Detroit."

"Downtown?"

"Sure."

I handed him two of Cindy's twenty dollar bills and his taxi rolled forward into my unsettled future.

CHAPTER FIVE

As the self slowly isolates the outside world, so too should that self expect abrupt and vicious reciprocity.

F. Gregor Grabner

The next thing I knew, my down payment was used up. Must have dozed off. I cleared my head with a deep breath - the kind that used to wake up Beth in the morning. I observed the familiar night-time surroundings of Gratiot Avenue, just south of Eight Mile Road. We were driving into the heart of the fair city of Detroit. Shortly, we passed Seven Mile Road. Then on my left I saw and remembered Carmen's party store. When I was in high school, you were sold anything you could get onto the counter at Carmen's. It was the favorite, if not the only, beer stop for my graduating class.

The driver pulled over to the right side of the road into an expired, metered spot and said, "Forty dollars stops here, sir."

"Okay, but take me over there to Carmen's. I want to get something to eat and then another ride." I pointed and he was irritated by the request.

It amazed me how damned easy non-automotive products and/or services had it with clientele. Here I am, his customer, I've paid him in cash, and he's complaining overtly about my request. Taxi drivers! And computers? Imagine what would happen if your brand new car randomly crapped out, would not respond at all, and the only way to fix it was to stop, get out, disconnect the battery cable, and then reconnect it after a few seconds? This is the same as having to reboot a computer but people put up with incompatible and malfunctioning computer hardware and software all the time. If a new car performed this poorly, the owner would drop a nut, eventually both nuts. Perhaps it was time to regulate computers. After assorted eyebrow contortions, the taxi driver complied with my wish and drove the two hundred yards to Carmen's parking lot.

"Are you getting out?" he asked.

"Yes, but please wait for me. I've got to get a few things." I climbed out of the yellow taxi, hungry and sad, and took the hard drive with me into the store. You never know about taxi drivers. There were bars on all of the windows. Inside, it still resembled the grubby party hovel I remembered. Three walls were lined with coolers chock-full of soda pop and various brands of courage made from hops or grapes. The fourth wall, directly across from the entrance, held the liquor and the cash registers, which were well protected behind one-inch-thick Plexiglas. I located a cold quart of Budweiser beer and hungered briefly for frog legs. I settled for an old turkey-loaf submarine sandwich. It was in the cooler by the rotating thing where money and goods were exchanged. These guys didn't sell ham. I paid and exited.

Outside, my loyal coachman had left me high and dry. A selective taxi driver. Didn't he see my roll of Cindy's twenties? Perhaps it was my outfit, designed for spying. There was no way of knowing his motives for certain. On the big clock outside the bank on the opposite side of Gratiot, I saw that it was 10.52 P.M. It was Thursday.

I sat down on a parking block in front of Carmen's and opened the aged sandwich. It was so old that the acid from the tomatoes had reacted with the oils of the Swiss cheese and dressing. They had all fused in a strange way. Dijon mustard, available in little tin foil packets on the customer side of the Plexiglas wall, fixed all that. I tore the corners off two of them and spread the contents on the sandwich. With no less homage to Frederick Henry, I proceeded to concentrate only on eating and drinking. There was no mortar fire that evening in Detroit. About six bites and thirty-two ounces later, I was content.

In the local media, the fair city of Detroit continued to get an unfair rap for crime and burnt-out, empty neighborhoods. But give Mayor Dennis Archer some time. He turned down a sure presidential cabinet post to stay in Detroit – a politician with integrity. I kept telling myself this as I walked on the east side of Gratiot into the bowels of Detroit past boarded up store fronts and sincere panhandlers. I simply wanted a taxi that would accept unmarked twenties. Times were difficult.

Then a southbound cab pulled over to the curb after completing a U-turn. My eyebrows were raised and my stomach slightly ached. It was a familiar car and I climbed in.

"Greyhound bus station near Howard Street and the Lodge, please." This I communicated rapidly and finished before I even sat down. The driver turned around and his substantial eyebrows were raised. It was the same driver who had abandoned me earlier! We realized this simultaneously and he looked sheepish. I felt like vomiting, yet remained curious.

"Why did you leave me at Carmen's?"

"I am very sorry about that, sir." Silence.

"That's it?" I replied. "Did I or did I not pay you cash?"

"Yes. Yes, you did, sir, but I was convinced that you were going to rob that party shop and I am no getaway driver. I'm on parole and cannot take chances."

"What?" My innards rumbled, protesting the old turkey and beer. And then I abruptly blew a huge pie (threw up) on his back seat to my left. The taxi cab was filled with smelly silence. Then: "You have vomited in my cab!"

I closed my eyes and leaned back. "Do you know of a quarter car-wash anywhere close? Those vacuums pick up everything."

"You are offering to pay for cleaning?"

"Sure?" I felt very bad, but the cab smelled much worse.

"What did you eat, sir?" he asked nicely. Woozy, I did not reply. No more than two minutes later we pulled into a quarter car-wash and I felt very queasy. I got out of the cab. There was no denying it —food poisoning. One must never count on cold cuts twice in one day for nourishment. I let go again, this time into a garbage can next to the high-powered vacuum. My stomach was empty. I was a mere shell of a test engineer.

Meanwhile, the driver made his way to the trunk, where a complete set of cleaning supplies and disinfectants were stored, including several rolls of paper towels. I came around a little, wandering about, and tried to help, inserting two quarters into the vacuum. After I sucked up the big pieces, he carefully attacked the seat with gobs of 409 and blathered on about things he was not paid enough to do. I dry-heaved in the direction of the garbage can, produced nothing, and said very, very little. I noticed that his meter continued to run and it clicked to twenty dollars just as he finished wiping down the seat.

We both got back into the yellow taxi, which pulled back out onto a road that I still cannot remember the name of, and shortly thereafter I was feeling sicker. Then, sometime later, I do not remember how long, the Greyhound bus station of original interest appeared. The driver politely demanded thirty dollars and my exit. The transaction occurred and I fell out of the taxi, with the hard drive, onto the walk alongside the wall of the bus depot. My situation was decreasing. People bustled past and looked curiously at me. I dry-heaved while lying on the cool concrete. Strangers were discussing where were the goddamn police when you needed them?

The ground moved and it was not an earthquake. Somebody threw a quarter and a nickel at me (based on my best recollection of the sound the coins made as they hit the concrete) and commented about a tough go of it. It was very blurry and I dry-heaved again, my body convulsing to empty an already empty stomach. Everybody spread out away from me like when a fight starts in a crowd.

"You all right, man?" he asked, holding my dark shirt while waving an ammonia capsule under my nose.

"Where am I?"

"Security office, Detroit Greyhound depot."

"How long have I been here?"

"Fifteen minutes. You done passed out cold on the sidewalk." The room was yellow and my stomach continued to flutter.

"Are there any busses going south tonight? I have to get going."

"You in no shape to travel, man. Are you on somethin'?"

"I had some bad turkey about an hour ago," I answered.

"Whoa. What gives with bad turkey? I ain't never heard of that. What is it, freebased whisky and crack or somethin'?"

"It's stinking rotten cold cuts!"

"I don't know how you could even smoke that stuff."

"Food poisoning. I've got food poisoning!" This security guard and I communicated poorly. Perhaps he knew Beth.

"Do you know Beth Drachman?" I asked for no plausible reason.

"No. An hour ain't long enough for food poisoning to set in," he said correctly. I thought about the ham sandwich at K-Mart and imagined another poor sot blowing pies like me. Regardless of the specific cause, I felt terrible.

"Well, man, it's my job, so I already called an ambulance. They can help you."

"What? I have no time for that." Just raising my voice a bit with this helpful man sapped my strength. "What time for a southbound bus tonight?"

"Midnight we got a bus headin' down I-75. Get you to Miami in thirty-two hours. Someday I'm gonna go there," he proclaimed, and released my shirt.

"I'm not going to Miami."

"That's no problem man, cause that bus is gonna stop in many a city along I-75. You just take your pick. But I'm goin' to Miami someday."

"That's nice."

"Since you ain't shot or nothin', the ambulance won't be here for a while. Sure you're okay?"

"More or less. Ambulance? I don't need an ambulance. Could I get some water?"

"Sure, no problem. There's a fountain out by the ticket booth."

"Where is that?"

"Follow the signs. And don't forget this thing." He handed me the precious piece of computer hardware. I stood up and fell down immediately, clutching it. The room spun around. He (I never got his name) helped me get up and I staggered slowly and used the walls for guidance. He was right about the signs.

The ticket to Dayton that I needed was twenty-nine dollars, but just in case I was still being followed and asked about, I bought a one-way to Atlanta for sixty-five dollars. Paranoia had served me well and it was crucial to keep them guessing. I paid for the ticket, enjoyed a long drink of water, sat down, and waited to board the southbound bus.

Wil Porter, a very brilliant friend I met at Michigan Tech many years ago, had recently completed his doctorate in electrical engineering at the University of Michigan. He had then taken a faulty, I mean faculty (see what a single letter can do to a word?) position at the University of Dayton in the electrical engineering department. Wil knew more about computer hardware than anybody I had ever met. Perhaps he could figure out how to get to whatever was hidden on the Bennington hard drive.

I believed something was there, otherwise nothing made sense. It seemed impossible that just two days ago my life was headed in the right direction - the best ever. Cindy Salome was very beautiful and smart, and she only nagged a little. And there was much more business with GM on the horizon. Sure, there were divorce details, but with the help of Ben David Fisher, they would soon be resolved. But I couldn't even call him anymore after carjacking his intern, Brook Taberman. It all seemed intolerable. I needed to talk to Cindy or Andy, or somebody with more knowledge than me.

I thought about how the federal government might be involved. Maybe Dirk Mott had further insight. He was a local talk radio personality who I listened to when I needed a laugh. Dirk Mott said he would only burn the American flag if it were time to overthrow the government to protect the Constitution.

I located a payphone and dialed Andy's number, collect. The water rumbled around in my stomach. It had been a long time since water sickened me. The automated operator told me to state my name, which I did. Shortly, I heard a busy signal and the drone-like electronic voice said the call could not be completed, please try again later. At least he's home, I thought.

The loudspeaker announced that the bus to Miami was Leaving in ten minutes, board now. But I dry-heaved. This one was very bile flavored. Yum. Then I realized how shitty and disgusting my mouth felt, so I found a bathroom and cleaned it out with soap. In the mirror was a fucking stranger! I could not believe how absolutely horrible I looked. There were bags and blotches and wrinkles everywhere on my previously reasonably handsome face. It was bad. This sight added greatly to a growing sense of desperation.

There were two things I had always taken for granted: good looks (not quite the Tom Cruise level, where a woman looks and thinks: I want to show him; but more like Jeff Daniels, where a woman looks and thinks: I suppose I don't mind showing him) and brains (I believed I was smarter than them). Since I had not experienced a clear thought in two days, I knew the brains part was on temporary hold. But that awful-looking man in the mirror was alarming. Then the little speaker over the mirror announced that Miami-bound passengers needed to board immediately.

Ever since my grandpa told me that God would never give me more or less than I could handle, I believed with all of my heart that he was right. Yet, at that moment, I wondered how in the world had I gotten into this mess; a Richard Kimble synonym. Did it start with the car accident up north?

It was necessary to talk to Andy Brooks to find out if he had had Ian Hatley beat to shit. That was a good starting point. But even if he did, why were all these people still after me? I realized why I had put off contacting him. And all those questions Cindy Salome and Officer Munday kept asking. Last call for Miami. Thank God.

The line of people waiting to get on the bus illustrated a clear demarcation of the haves and the have-nots in our great society. Where was Lyndon Johnson? In recent months, thanks to Burt Morgan, I had been able to travel first class or business class everywhere I went. All of my travel was work-related. The last time I rode a bus was during freshmen year at Michigan Tech. I took a Greyhound round-trip for Christmas break. That was two years before Mike had enrolled with me to take on Eli Whitney. Each direction took seventeen hours. I forgot that people with little extra money used Greyhound. I shuffled along in line, clutching the hard drive, further understanding my plight, and showed my boarding pass.

The last row on the bus was empty. After handing my boarding pass to the pissed off driver, I lurched back there to sleep, hopefully. Seated, I noticed a familiar man in the row just in front of me. At the time, he was difficult to place, but it would soon come to me. The other seven or eight passengers sat towards the front of the bus. Apparently, not many people went south in June.

The bus wheeled out of the depot and passed directly in front of John King used books, the largest store of its kind in Michigan. I turned my head and looked out the rear window at the depot, thinking about Richard Kimble when he first saw the one-armed man leaving on the bus. But there was nothing there to count on, nobody to see me off. And worse, David Janssen was dead. The bus turned left onto the northbound Lodge freeway, then to I-94 east, then to I-75 south. I was on my way.

From all accounts, it appeared that my vomiting phase was over. There was nothing more to throw. Although I still felt queasy, I fell asleep and dreamt about that fellow in the row in front of me. I may have awakened at the Toledo stop, or maybe some city between Toledo and Dayton (my memory fails me), but I definitely remember people getting on and off. And that fellow in front of me stayed put. Why? Why? Because I hit him in the head with my valise! He was on the jet I rode back from Arizona two days ago. Today, however, he wore a fake mustache! It could not be a coincidence; he was following me!

Since I was not driving, crashing into a tall concrete wall was no option. An internal debate about what exactly to do ensued. One part of me said, be up front, tell him what's happened to you. Then I considered Saddam Hussein's two sons-in-law. They told all and were cut in half upon their heroic return to Baghdad. I briefly considered choking to death the small man in the next row, but decided that it was impractical.

Moving slowly while faking sleep, I pulled my belt from around my waist. I sat directly behind him.

The driver called out, "Dayton terminal, next stop! About ten minutes!"

The small, blue-eyed man in front of me did not react.

Still feigning sleep, I slowly looped the belt back through the buckle, forming a noose. Without hesitation, I extended my arms and put the noose around his neck and pulled tight. Very tight. Hit man, G-man, or fellow spy, that night he was a stunned mortal, just like the rest of us.

He froze and gasped for air and I let up a little to tell him I wanted his cooperation in return for his life. He knew that I was onto him and would certainly kill him if he tried to lead. He stopped struggling. People in the front part of the bus heard the commotion and looked back, perplexed, straining their necks. With my right hand pushing on the back of his chair for leverage and my left hand on the noose, he stood no chance of escape. He had to cooperate. Who says test engineers are predictable?

"You and I are going slowly to the front of the bus," I told him quietly.

He tried to speak but sounded like a warm can of beer opening. I thought I was pulling too tight, but held firm.

"Slowly," I repeated, noticing that he had no luggage with him. I also knew that spies did not check luggage. Then I moved my right hand to the center of his upper back and snugged up the noose again. I told him to put his left hand behind his back. He did so and I grasped the wrist and pushed it hard, up and in between his shoulder blades. I grabbed his shirt to help anchor my hold on his arm. This made it harder for him to spin his body away. He tried nothing. I led him like we were dancing and he followed well. His right hand floated by his side, refusing to fight. I felt like Bluto before Popeye had his spinach. We walked toward the front of the bus and I assured the other passengers along the way that things were under complete control.

"Just stay calm folks. I'm an undercover police officer. This man has a bomb under his shirt."

Gasps of "Oh no!" and "Oh my God" sprang from the crowd, and the man I was choking wriggled a little with disapproval.

We arrived at the front of the bus.

"Driver!" I demanded. "Stop this bus, immediately."

The driver complied, and we pulled off to stop on the right side of the interstate. "Now, when I say to open the door, do it. And then close it when I say."

"All right, mister." But he was not convinced of my status as a lawman.

"Open it!"

Swiftly, I half pushed and half threw the small man down the steps through the open doorway. And I kicked his legs so that he crashed hard, face down, onto the gravel along I-75.

"Close the door and put it to the floor before that psycho ignites the bomb!"

Again, the driver complied.

I grabbed the shiny vertical pole by the driver for balance.

The bus sped off, leaving the man gasping for air, and, no doubt, very angry.

"You're crazy," he indicated.

"That may be true, sir," I announced to him and all passengers, "but you have very likely just saved the lives of these people." I spread my hands out like a preacher and continued, "Let's all give the driver here... what is your name, sir?"

"Ike."

"Ike, let's give Ike here a round of applause."

The weak clapping sounds tapered off quickly. Then a woman on the bus said, "Let's see your badge."

"Undercover, we don't carry a badge. Safety purposes, so we don't get burned."

She paused, then replied, "Oh, that's right. I remember from that TV show *Wiseguy*. Okay, never mind. Thank God you were on board!"

One born every day, I thought, smiling at her.

But the driver looked doubtful.

"As a matter of fact," I went on, "I do need to get off up here so I can notify the appropriate authorities."

"I can call the police from here," said the driver.

"This is bigger than the police. Stop here and let me off. I'll take care of it. You just get these fine people to Dayton, or to wherever they're headed."

The driver looked perplexed, still doubtful, but slowed to a stop, again.

Throwing that guy off the bus was cathartic. But I had to assume that he had a cell phone and notified his superiors, who would then be waiting for me at the bus terminal in Dayton. We had driven a few miles, and I chose to risk that I would not encounter him along the side of the interstate. Also, if he hitched a ride from someone, I concluded that he would either follow after the bus or not see me walking. There was no doubt that his intention at the Detroit bus depot was to follow me and do something. Caution was still needed. I half smiled and returned to the rear of the bus to retrieve the hard drive, then I confidently strode to the front and exited.

The bus door closed behind me and the vehicle drove off, blending into traffic very swiftly. Walking along the shoulder of 1-75, thinking about Beth and Ed

Finninen and feeling sick from the bad turkey, the dark June air was moist and comfortably cool. It felt safe.

The bigger question of finding Wil Porter and engaging his help remained. In the distance, there was a Holiday Inn. The only way to it was via the next exit ramp, about two miles away. I continued on. About thirty minutes later, carrying the hard drive and a worsening attitude, the dingy, poorly run inn approached. I entered the lobby and addressed the night clerk.

"I need a room. Just me. Best rate."

A young, pretty woman wearing imitation Oliver Peoples glasses looked up. "What again?"

"I need your least expensive room for one night."

"Smoking or non?"

"Non."

Sighs and rapid computer keystrokes followed. "Okay, 302 is available for forty-nine."

"How much?"

"Forty-nine dollars, sir."

"That's quite a bit," I protested. "Have you considered that it is early Friday morning?"

"What again?"

"It's past midnight and very unlikely that anybody else will buy the room."

"I know that. What's your point?"

"Will you accept thirty dollars?"

"No, sir. I know your kind," she replied keenly. "The rate is forty-nine."

"At midnight, the rate is whatever somebody will pay," I replied. But she did not get it.

"No sirree. It says right here that 302 costs forty-nine dollars on weekdays in June."

I was weary. "Is the manager in?"

"You are looking at the night manager," she said proudly. No wonder Holiday Inns have gone to shit.

"Let me try to explain," I began. "If you don't sell this room tonight, how much will you make on it?" She smiled and rolled her eyes playfully.

"Nothing, obviously. God."

"Right. Now, if you sell it for forty-nine, about how much do you make on it?"

"About thirty dollars."

"That makes sense. So, if you make thirty bucks when the room sells for forty-nine, forget about taxes and stuff, that means the room costs about twenty dollars to prepare per day, right?"

"Well, let me see. Rosie and Cookie split sixteen dollars per room cleaned. That's subject to inspection, naturally. Those Haitians don't go the extra mile, if you get my meaning. And the little soaps and laundry cost about three dollars, depending on how dirty the sheets are." She paused. "All right then, about twenty dollars. Can you believe that some people have actually asked for hourly rates?" She looked appalled, but fully confident.

"Good." My patience was thinning. "So, if you sell the room for thirty dollars, how much do you make?"

"But the rate is forty-nine!" she insisted.

"I know that. I know. But think about things differently, like Joel Barker."

"Who?"

"A guy I know. Never mind. What's your name?"

"Crystal Sue."

"Okay then, Crystal —"

"Crystal Sue," she interrupted. "I just hate that. What's your name?"

"Frank."

"Well then, Fran. See what I mean? My whole life people calling me Crystal. The name is Crystal Sue." Her point was made.

"Crystal Sue then. Consider what you would make if you sold the room for thirty dollars. And forget about taxes and stuff - they apply to any price."

"Well," she pondered, "it would be thirty minus twenty. This hotel would make just ten dollars in such a situation."

"That's right."

"But the rate is still forty-nine," she said.

Another approach was needed. "What are the chances that you will turn people away tonight because you're full?"

"Oh, God. Zero chance of that. We never sell out except on some weekends."

"That, Crystal Sue, is exactly my point. Do you want to make zero or ten dollars, on room 302?"

Her bright blue eyes squinted and her brow furrowed up, moving light brown bangs, which gently touched her glasses. She smelled nice too. "The new rate for 302 is thirty-five dollars, taxes included," she replied calmly, finally learning this basic point. This Holiday Inn might just survive. They could get Jean-Claude Killy to endorse.

"Deal." I filled out that little card, paid thirty-five dollars, and started off to the room, completely tired. But before leaving the lobby, I asked Crystal Sue for the Holiday Inn's total care package: toothbrush, razor, and deodorant. She said, smiling, that it was free today only.

"Thank you, Crystal Sue." I went back out and found room 302, which faced southbound I-75, entered, drank some water, brushed my teeth, and fell asleep.

I awoke at about 7.30 A.M. and felt rested. My stomach was still fluttering, but it was much better. I did my business on the toilet, cleared my brains as Andy Brooks would say. I still needed to call him. I showered.

Refreshed and combed, I left the room key on the TV, thought of Beth and Ed, and walked out to the road in front of the Holiday Inn. There were over six hundred dollars (and change) remaining of Cindy's money. I walked for a few minutes away from the interstate, flagged down the first available taxi, climbed in, and requested a ride to the University of Dayton. I was hungry but had no appetite.

It was a beautiful Friday morning in June in southern Ohio. And I was a fugitive.

CHAPTER SIX

Open-ended life not so bad.

Pavel Botchkov

For no good reason, I felt safe in the taxi and paid little attention to my precise surroundings. We drove for about five minutes.

The driver said, "Sir, do you have a particular building in mind?"

"Engineering or electrical engineering. Either one," I replied.

Depending on the size of a school, different engineering disciplines like electrical, mechanical, or chemical had their own buildings. The University of Dayton was not a large university, but because of its proximity to Wright Patterson Airbase and the resultant military/academic partnerships, all areas of engineering had evolved during the cold war into solidly average programs, in the Michigan Tech sense. Of course, in respective hometowns, these types of engineering universities were simply the best.

The undergraduate engineering program at Dayton had grown too quickly, just like Michigan Tech's Eli Whitney School of Engineering. To remedy this, the Dayton trustees, just like Michigan Tech's trustees, decided that adding an underfunded graduate program was the only way to make such an overpopulated undergraduate college feasible. This way, reasonably competent, underpaid graduate students could teach very large sophomore level engineering classes for much less than it would cost to have the marginally competent, tenured faculty members teach them. Similar to a cotton gin, the bad seeds (students) could then be cheaply separated from the pack and discarded along with their dreams and the dreams of those who loved them. This allowed the tenured faculty to continue with their research, while simultaneously minimizing their teaching responsibilities. All in all, it was a very clever technique for maintaining the status quo in the American engineering education process.

In one key way, Dayton's electrical engineering department was an exception: it had developed nationally recognized programs in electro-optics and computers. Both graduate and undergraduate programs were very good, even compared to the famous electrical engineering schools like MIT, Berkeley, and Illinois. Given this, the University of Dayton was a perfect fit for the computer genius Wil Porter, and he was happy working there.

After a few moments of silence, the taxi driver basically claimed ignorance about where the buildings might be located, but of course he was willing to drive around for as long as necessary to find them.

I concluded that America's taxi drivers were better trained in marketing than in directions.

"How about Physics or Mathematics, or anything close?" I asked. He sighed and nodded, then proceeded directly to the Physics building. The taxi stopped and I handed the driver ten dollars for a fare less than that, and exited. I was feeling like a big shooter, an uncaught man on the run. It was fun.

The campus was nice: liberal, but alive because of conservative money. There were people walking in and out of the old, brick Physics building.

I approached a very focused Samoan student and addressed him. "Excuse me, where is the engineering or electrical engineering building?"

He looked up from the invisible yellow brick road he was following and pointed behind me, over the top of my head, and said, "There's a big sign in front of electrical engineering. If you miss it, you need a dog."

"Thanks." Under my breath I mumbled something further that ended in a hole. My mind leaped...

The problem with Cindy and the night Ian Hatley was beaten was that I went out to Burger King at 11.30 P.M. and did not get back until well after midnight. The drive-thru by her place was closed and I spent half an hour just trying to find one that was open. In the process, I got a damned speeding ticket - at 12.09 A.M.! I wonder how long it took Officer Munday to discover that? Hapless, I hoped that Cindy had told the police she was with me in the car. I never told her about the ticket (I don't know why). It was raining that night and I thought that pulling over and walking back to the police car (so that the officer would not get wet) would reduce my risk of receiving a ticket. Nope. On the plus side, however, that officer could not truthfully testify that I was alone in the car. Ha! My mind leaped back...

I walked the length of about two football fields, read the large sign, and proceeded up the concrete steps. Inside, the old, pompous building had brand new, painful, purple and green checkered tile floors. All around were young, tired, optimistic people shuffling briskly to their eight o'clock summer term classes. I was caught in the flow like a big log in a fast river. Several more steps into the building, on the wall, was a bulletin board littered with party announcements and Dianetics workshop dates. One of the flyers asked the question: *Was L. Ron Hubbard the Son of God?* And I thought, isn't he dead? I could not believe that people were stupid enough to even consider such bullshit, let alone send money!

Next to the bulletin board was a cabinet with locked glass doors that contained the names and office numbers of electrical engineering faculty. Wil Porter was in Room 226. After a quick deduction, I strolled to the stairway that was about twenty feet away and walked up. The second floor looked just like the first floor except near the windows (different view). Following the numbers, I located Wil's office. His schedule, a multicolored, weekly grid with teaching assignments, office hours, and research times carefully noted, was thumbtacked in each corner to the wooden door. On this Friday morning, Wil was teaching a digital electronics course from eight to nine.

Full of beer and bullshit at the Doghouse Saloon in Houghton (Michigan Tech was in Houghton), Wil and I would argue about where the future of electrical engineering was going. I thought that microwave communications and electromagnetic compatibility would lead the way. Wil predicted that computers were the main area and probably would remain so for many decades. Consideration of who was asking who for help, I concluded quickly that Wil was correct. But still, I only partly believed it (pride, perhaps).

Although a top-notch risk taker, I was weak at foresight (as my current situation supports). I acted first and thought thoroughly later. Wil, unnaturally, had the best of both skills. He could work through potential consequences very rapidly, as only the brilliant can. His mind worked extremely fast and he was patient with his results. For example, if Wil was convinced that his marriage was over on Tuesday, he would not move out on Wednesday, as I would. He would take a step back and perhaps go to counseling for a while with his future ex-spouse, all the while knowing. Once it became clear to her too that it was really over (it is nonsense that one half of a marriage deep down believes that it is good enough to keep alive, while the other half does not) she would feel less angry and scorned (in some cases). In a divorce, Wil would get a better financial settlement than me. Of course, he would have to get married first.

According to the posted schedule, he would return at 9.00 A.M. for office hours. Since my stomach was growling and cramping from hunger and residual food poisons, and there was almost a full hour to wait, I decided to find some breakfast. I walked around the building in search of a vending machine, which I found and which contained peanut M&Ms. Again, though, unmarked twenties were my curse: not enough change and no singles. If, for forty-five minutes, I sat patiently, hungry, for Wil's return, I'd be cranky and hard to work with. When blood sugar drops, so does everything else. Accordingly, I found my way back outside and bumped into a waif-like woman as tall as me. She had short, flaming-red hair.

"Excuse me," I said, "do you know where I can find the union?"

"It all starts in your heart," she answered, waiting for me to reply.

"No, no. Not that kind of union. I'm hungry."

"As we all are." She had bright blue eyes and I thought about her.

"What are you hungry for? Are you a philosophy major?" I her asked lightly.

"No, industrial engineering."

"Well, then I'll try again. Where is the student union? I'm assuming that it has a cafeteria."

"I knew what you meant the first time. And yes, it does have one."

"Then why did —"

"My humanities professor said that nine out of ten times when a stranger asks you something that you interpret as a bigger question, when it's really not, the stranger will inquire further, as though you had answers. You're in the minority," she said, then smiled.

I could not help smiling back. "What course is this?" I asked.

"Twentieth-century American culture."

"Sounds like a good one."

"It is."

"I am really hungry. Could you direct me to the union?"

"Sure." She smiled again and pointed behind me and over my head.

Before I ask anybody else here for directions, I'm going to look behind me first, I thought. Then I thought about her more.

"Do you want to get some breakfast?" I asked. What did I have to lose?

"Any other time I would, but I'm really late for a class. But thanks for being a data point." She turned and was off, shoulders level, never to be seen again by me.

I thought about her all the way to the cafeteria and through a buffet breakfast of eggs, bacon, toast, and orange juice. Infatuation was more appropriate after I cleared my name. I finished eating and started back to Wil Porter's office. Along the way, I switched my thinking back to what was happening, arrived and waited outside his door, tapping my left foot. I noticed the hard drive in my right hand. For most of the morning I had held onto it subconsciously.

Wil Porter approached his office at 9.00 A.M. sharp. From the thirty or so paces between us, we recognized each other; Wil had gained a little weight and I looked like shit. It had been a while since we last saw each other, but we had talked many times on the phone.

At our last encounter, I introduced him to my test lab and staff (Andy Brooks), and he seemed impressed by it all. After the tour, Wil, Andy, and I went to Lelli's restaurant, the one by the Pontiac Silverdome, for lunch. I paid the bill and Wil was impressed further. Now, though, I was impressed by his situation. Whenever I asked about co-eds and faculty, Wil would only say, "Remember Donald Sutherland in Animal House?" The scoundrel. After lunch at Lelli's, Wil started back to Dayton, and Andy and I went back to Forward Research and Test. On the way, Andy said he'd bet that Wil and Mike were a lot alike. I said nothing and Andy didn't pursue it.

I said to my approaching friend, "Wil Porter, computer genius!"

"Drachman, don't tell me I've still got you fooled!" He replied heartily.

It was really great to see him. "How the hell are you?" I asked back.

"Heavier and better than you look. Pardon my frankness, Frank, but you look like crap! What's going on?"

"A long story." Although I tended to be dramatic (according to Beth), I deeply sighed without trying.

Some students in the area who obviously knew Wil from a class noticed our discussion and hung around to observe.

Then I continued, "Can we go in your office?"

We entered and I held the hard drive and closed the door and Wil spoke first.

"Andy Books called me yesterday and asked if I had seen you. He told me about you and Beth. How did he know you'd come to see me?"

"I don't know."

"Are you and Beth splitting up?"

"It sure looks that way."

"I thought you two would make it through anything."

"Sorry I let you down."

"I didn't mean that; it's surprising though. What's up?"

"Is that all Andy told you?"

"No. He mentioned something about a murder, but then said he had to go before the call was traced. Doesn't he know that when you call out, the phone company can immediately identify who you're calling?"

"I guess not."

"Who is Ian Hatley?"

"Don't you mean who was Ian Hatley?" I corrected.

"Right."

I proceeded to tell Wil Porter five chapters of details. He listened intently for over an hour, intermittently answering timid knocks on his door and telling students that they would have to come back, sorry.

"That must be the hard drive then," he commented, pointing to the thing on my lap.

"That is it," I replied.

He picked it up. "It's a Seagate," Wil began, with the intensity of sure knowledge filling him. "About twenty-five millisecond access time. Kind of slow and old. Capacity's about a hundred megabytes. But it's a good, reliable unit."

"Great. Is there any way to hide data on it so that Norton Utilities can't find it?"

"I suppose so. But I'll have to take it to my lab downstairs to check it out. Let's go." On the way the lab, Wil asked what I was expecting or hoping to find. I told him I didn't know. We continued walking and hall clocks registered 10.16 A.M. Time was running as fast as a frightened goose.

Shortly, we arrive at Wil's computer lab. The entrance door had a long, narrow window next to the doorknob. He fumbled with a densely-populated key ring and unlocked the door. We entered. Inside the room were many, many cobbled-up computers; half of one connected to half of another, yet still workable. It looked like Frankenputer.

"Come over here, Frank." Wil turned left once inside the door and walked rapidly toward a cluttered workbench. He had been filling up with that thing geniuses have the instant I told him data recovery was needed. He had a passion for answers that was second to nothing I had ever seen as a test-for-profit engineer. He cleared a pile of wires and circuit boards off the wooden bench top, reached underneath and pulled out a laptop similar in vintage to the one I owned. I held onto the hard drive. He wordlessly prompted me for it.

"Can you interface to the drive?" I asked.

"Sure." In about one minute, Wil had dismantled his computer and connected up my decrepit unit. He waited for the boot-up impatiently, now fully in his driven mode. All parts of the computer – the monitor, the keyboard, the RAM, the hard drive – were communicating, exchanging information millions of times per second. I heard and saw rapid keystrokes and thought of Crystal Sue at the Holiday Inn. A few moments passed.

"There are no ASCII files hidden on this drive," he said confidently.

"It seemed that way when I bought it. Are you sure there's no other way to hide them?"

Wil raised his left brow, apparently surprised that I would question his disc-checking program.

I continued, "That's the confusing part. But a lot of people are after this thing and I know something is on it."

"How do you know that?"

"Like I told you, somebody was murdered and I was almost killed."

"Well, I hate to tell you, but there are no hidden files on this thing. Are you sure there's nothing else to go on?"

"To be straight, Wil, I don't know and I have nowhere else to turn. Beth and I are separated. And she's already screwing somebody. Do you remember Ed Finninen?"

"From Tech?"

"Yes, I think so. Tall, quiet. Well, its him." I paused, thinking again about Beth and Ed. "In a way it really is my fault."

"How's that?"

"I haven't really talked to anybody about this, but I sort of went back on a promise I made to Beth."

"A Promise?"

"Yup. We had a deal. If we couldn't survive on my income from Forward Research and Test when it came time for us to start a family, which was last December according to our plans, then I would pack in the self-employed bit and find a job with a bigger company like GM or Ford. The benefits and job security they offer are really tough to beat, especially for a mediocre test engineer. Beth wanted to stay at home with the kids and I sort of liked that."

"Don't underestimate yourself. You helped lots of people with homework at Tech, including me. So, you two were going to start a family?" He asked genuinely.

"We were. I was able to get Beth to agree to wait six or eight months when the GM blanket opportunity came up, but she resented it. She turned thirty this past February and did not want to wait. I think she wanted me to fail. I could just tell."

"But she agreed to wait to see if the GM thing paid off."

"She did, but not without a price. She reminded me every day. After three months of it, I started to feel like an unwilling sperm donor. I may have broken a promise, but it wasn't like I didn't want a family. I just needed another year or so to get in solid with

GM. I realized that she didn't give two shits about what I wanted."

"From starting a family to getting a divorce. A great divide."

"Sure was. I mean hey, if I couldn't keep a promise about a family, then what did any promise mean? Those were her words. It really got to me. After she agreed to wait six or eight months, nothing I did was ever enough. I got sick of it. It made looking around a lot easier. Who needs constant nagging?" But I still felt guilty and looked for reprieve.

"Not one man that I know," replied Wil dryly.

"Anyway, all it really did was expose a crippling weakness in our relationship. Better now than when Junior is in grade school. Besides, Beth can find someone else; she's still great looking and all that."

"Drachman, you're in denial. Ed Finninen?"

"Oh right. Right. You're right. She's already located someone else." I felt bad discussing it.

"Finninen's married, right?" asked Wil.

"Last time I read the Michigan Tech Alumni magazine he was married to the girl he met at Tech, Christy something or other."

"Maybe Christy will go out with you," he joked.

It felt worse, but I knew Wil was just trying to lighten things up. "Maybe she will," I replied.

"I'm sorry, Frank."

I nodded acceptingly and said, "I don't want to involve you in this mess any more than I already have. Disconnect that thing and I'll be on my way.

I'll try to keep you in the loop, but if you don't hear from me for a few months, watch the news."

"What are you going to do?"

"The only thing I can: go back to Michigan, try to figure out what everybody is after, and hope for the best."

He listened while dismantling the cobbled array of electronics. He extracted my hard drive and held it for my taking. "Here you go, Frank."

"Thanks. And to think life would depend on a Seagate hard drive." I took the device and looked at it from several angles and incorrectly scoffed, "I'll bet the serial number adds up to a fricking multiple of thirteen."

Then Wil looked closely again at the drive. "That's funny, Frank, but you might have something. Notice that the so-called serial number has ten digits?"

"And?"

"Well, this is a Seagate drive!" Wil exclaimed, presuming as all geniuses do, that the answer was obvious.

"All right already, Wil. So what?"

"Seagate uses seven digit serial numbers."

"Are you saying that this is a false serial number?"

"I'm saying that it is not a real Seagate serial number."

"Let me copy the damn numbers and leave this relic with you," I said, locating a piece of paper and a pencil on Wil's crowded bench. I scribbled the numbers: 1424679698.

"That's fine with me. Maybe there's something I missed," he replied, smiling, knowing full well that he had missed nothing. I put the piece of paper in my right front pants' pocket.

"Well, I've got to go. Thanks for your help, Wil. I don't know what else to say."

"Neither do I. Sorry to hear about you and Beth. And good luck with this thing. Damn it, Frank, I really don't know what else to say either."

We shook hands firmly and I went out into the hallway, down the stairs and outside. It was turning into a very nice day and I walked along the street, surrounded by ambitious students and mostly second-rate academics. I needed a payphone. I walked for about ten minutes to the edge of the campus and found one.

I suddenly shifted into Frank Drachman, test-for-profit engineer mode, and wondered if the lab's best man, Andy, had kept working in my absence. I hoped that the untested and unplanned crisis management schemes of Forward Research and Test were operating adequately – whatever they might be. After all, there was a certain momentum that a business like mine maintained. At least for a while.

Perhaps Andy had finished the FCC radio frequency (RF) emissions test for Saturn's built-in TV/navigation module. Anybody in automotive electrical design knew that if a piece of electronic equipment mounted on a car generated electromagnetic emissions near or a little greater than commercial FCC levels, then whoever drove that car would hear the interference on the radio. So, for the sake of customer satisfaction, the auto companies had essentially self-regulated for years. Demonstrate that there is no need for regulations!

But in the case of Saturn's multi-function display, since it was removable and could be used outside the car, the FCC decided to flex its muscle and require formal compliance with the commercial FCC levels.

Although it would be tough to find in writing, it is clearly apparent to anyone who knows anything that when it comes to cars, certain people within the federal regulatory agencies (NHTSA, FCC, EPA, for example) all want to catch the big companies in violation of something so they can be on CNN or ABC, portrayed as necessary do-gooders. Most of these folks, like politicians and writers, care little about the good of the people, but more about their own egos and well-being. Perhaps they should be regarded as corrupt critics with too much authority.

In response to this accusation, the do-gooders say, "Look at how much safer cars are today than forty years ago."

And in response to that, any pre-production test engineer worth his salt would say, "I can see that."

But if we outlaw red meat and peanut M&Ms, then heart disease in forty years will be lower too. All in time. Thinking about work and unnecessary regulations upset me. Hey, perhaps I could sue the FCC for causing me emotional duress! I need Geoffrey Fieger! I decided to call Andy to see how my business was doing. Since I had memorized my MCI credit card number, no change was needed. This might have given away my location, but it was a risk I had decided to take.

Four rings later, "Good morning, Forward Research and Test," Andy said formally.

"Frank Drachman, please," I said, imitating Ronald Reagan's voice for no good reason.

"Mr. Drachman is out of town on business. It is an open-ended trip. Who's calling?"

"Well done, Andy!" I exclaimed in my regular voice.

"Frank?"

"It's me, Andy."

"I've had no idea where you've been. How in God's name are you?"

"Overall, I've been all right. Still lots of unanswered questions though. How is the testing business?" I asked. In the background of my mind, waiting for Andy's reply, I thought of the countless, comforting, distracting details associated with testing and measurement. And I remembered how Beth would tease me that if I was not handsome, then I would be a full-fledged dork. Some people liked to eat, some liked to drink, and still others focused on work. I preferred them all. I especially liked work; just the word, work, it was so tangible and self-sufficient. Then I turned back into Andy.

". . . and the test report went out yesterday to Saturn."

"The multi-function display results?" I asked.

"Yes, Frank. The one for Saturn. Are you okay?"

"I guess so. I'm trying to figure out how to resolve everything that's happened."

"The police, especially that Officer Munday, think you killed Ian Hatley. Or had him killed."

"I know."

"Well, did you?" he asked. It had been almost fifty years since Korea, but Andy had killed many men and still spoke about it as though it was somewhere between fishing and self-defense.

"No. but that's what I want to ask you."

"Me, Frank, why the hell would I kill somebody I've never met?"

"I don't know, Andy," I lied. "So, you had nothing to do with it?"

"Nothing."

"Has Officer Munday asked you about an alibi?"

"Yes. I was sleeping. I think she believes me, But I don't think she likes you too much. How about your alibi?"

"My head is spinning. There are many things to go into now. But I'm in—"

"That sounds good, Wil," he firmly interrupted. "Goodbye then." He hung up.

Evidently, Andy was doing his best to keep me from being traced. I hung up and looked several minutes for a taxi, which I located and hailed. There was no need for Andy to know I was going back to Michigan.

"Take me to the nearest Greyhound bus station," I told the driver.

"Yes, sir."

We arrived twenty minutes later. I had no sense of direction. The small, tanned driver requested fifteen dollars and I peeled off a twenty from the thick collection and told him to keep the change. I walked into the small building and got into the ticket line. A few minutes later, "When does the next bus to Flint, Michigan leave?"

"The daily to Traverse City will be through in about an hour," replied the round-faced, dedicated Greyhound employee.

"Give me a round-trip ticket then." I was very keen not to be detected. I paid the forty-two dollars and sat in the dingy terminal. There were about fifty seats and less than a quarter of them were full. Soon the bus arrived. I climbed aboard, feeling like a spy assigned to my own life.

CHAPTER SEVEN

Make no mistake about the permanency of skepticism.

Hunt Lange

As we proceeded onto northbound I-75, I looked out the window of the bus and dozed off and dreamt about many things. I awoke and checked the time with a fellow passenger, and over four hours had passed. I noted that Beth was on my mind, heavily, and Ed Finninen too. Fuck them, I thought, and again remembered vividly that they had covered that base. Then a little while later, we pulled into the main downtown Detroit terminal, the scene of another recent, personal incident. Remember the food poisoning? I decided to stay on board. The next stop was Royal Oak, then Pontiac, where I did get off. The bus depot there was located on the west side of Woodward just south of Orchard Lake Road. I thanked the driver and exited the bus.

Outside, breathing the fresh air, I developed a sudden urge to eat a cheeseburger at BO's microbrewery and grill. This establishment was located in the up-and-coming downtown area of

Pontiac, which was really making a rebound, just like Royal Oak did ten years ago. It felt good to anticipate supporting a place that was part of such a comeback, and so I began the ten minute walk from the bus station to BO's.

Walking hungry in the warm, late-afternoon sun, thinking about eating a cheeseburger loaded with onions, pickles, and mustard and drinking a cold beer, was almost as nice as doing it. I was growing less anxious about my overall situation. Like, I thought, when you run out of gas in unfamiliar territory. You putter to a stop along the roadside, fighting the inoperative power steering, your mind racing in agitation, park, and get out. If you don't have a cell phone with you, an open-ended walk for help is unavoidable. Strangely, the closeness of the competitive rubble, traffic, and surrounding environment actually becomes distracting enough to be relaxing. Similarly, I was more relaxed as a fugitive than I would have expected.

Shortly, I arrived at the doorstep of BO's and entered. A tall, backless bar stool seemed like a logical seat, so I sat down alone among empty backless bar stools along the bar on the right as I entered. I said "Hello" to the immediately approaching waitress. She was light-skinned and well proportioned, neither large nor small anywhere, and had about ten earrings in each ear. No matching pairs. Her face had all things just right. Her black, purple, and blonde striped hair supported my theory that Pontiac and Royal Oak had much in common, except for a few things that I cannot mention. There was no one else seated at the bar, but the bi-level restaurant (a main floor plus a loft set back from the bar that covered the kitchen) was about fifty percent full, smoky, and acoustically loaded with the flirtatious banter of a middle to late twenty-something lunch crowd.

Mainly, there were full tables of pretty, Mr. Goodbar-seeking young women (ten years ago I did not see it this way) checkered with tables of healthy looking, I'm Mr. Woodbar young men (ten years ago I did see it this way). Most of these guys were unaccomplished by capitalist standards and lived at home with a divorced parent, but were paying members of Gold's Gym or a similar institution of higher health. The girls loved them for reasons they did not understand. I thought quickly then turned to face the green-eyed bartendress.

"What can I get you?" she asked in a slight, pleasant, Jamaican accent.

"The keys to a new car and a million dollars," I replied.

"To drink?" she replied, bored by my attempt at humor. No facial reaction.

"What do you have on draft?" I replied. Hey, I could be remote and cool too.

"Well, we have several. This is a microbrewery you know," she said professionally, while pointing to the long selection list on the wall behind her written in large, fancy letters. I read the list, which included amber ale, summer bock, springtime red, BO's special pilsner/stout blend, cherry-cinnamon lite, and several others.

"Last time I was here Budweiser was on the list. Can I get one of those?"

"Sorry, we don't sell bottled domestics any longer. The big distributors are pulling back. We think it's because our beer makes their beer look and taste bad. They wanted to stop the side by side comparisons which, as you can imagine, happened all the time here." She was quite articulate and convincing, and even though I had not previously considered such a dynamic, I could now see her point.

"Have you ever considered going into hotel or restaurant management?" I asked genuinely.

She looked surprised, but still bored, and answered, "Yes, I have."

Okay, I thought, she's not really interested in talking. I can handle that. It's important to know when to quit, to keep your dignity. I glanced at her name tag.

"So, you're not very talkative today, are you Estelle?"

"No unfortunately, I'm not. What would you like, sir?" Pursed lips.

Time to quit. Really. "How about a medium-well cheddarburger and a summer bock?"

She listened, wrote, then turned towards the tap behind her and poured the beer slowly and served it. After that, she walked around to the front of the bar and across to the grill area and placed my order. I might have been staring at her, but it was sure easy to do.

I turned back towards the bar and a busboy popped up from a crouching position. "Hey bro, don't take it personal. Estelle's like that with just about every guy that comes in here. She's a real professional. She's going to Michigan State this fall to study hotel and restaurant management."

"I'm sure she'll do well."

"I'm Stan. My dad owns the place so I can always find a job," he smiled. "You know, we have a band coming on in ten minutes. I talked my dad into having a happy hour band. I hired these guys." He handed me a flyer:

The Shy
Detroit's Hottest Acoustic Rock Trio
Happy Hour at BO's
Every Friday
4.30 to 6.40 P.M.
Free Hot Snacks, No Cover

"Are they any good?" I asked.

"Absolutely. Effin' aye. Yes. They rock. They're like a cross between early acoustic Zeppelin and The Church. Only difference is The Shy's original drummer's not dead. He's tight. You know what else? The dude paints, too. This is no ordinary band. You know the bass player's got a friggin' doctorate degree in some language or linguistics shit? No shit. He's a smart dude."

"That's pretty impressive," I replied earnestly. I was never very big on college, couldn't wait to finish and get into the real world.

"Hey, ah, what is your name?"

"Frank."

"Between you and me, Frank, Estelle likes the lead singer. Guy plays the guitar and sings like it's two guys. He's awesome. They got a CD coming out too. And a website on Yahoo. Did I tell you this happy hour thing was my idea?"

"Yes, you did, Stan. Well at least she likes some guys."

"Who, Estelle?"

"Yes."

"It's the musicians. They always get the babes. Estelle's pretty hot, but she's got a kid. The singer's married anyway. Estelle was bummed. Her husband – I never met him – he got blown up in Desert Storm. They didn't even find his dog tags. I was studying music at Wayne State. Hadda quit though. Just not cut out for college."

Stan was very friendly and talkative. His pupils were huge and he had dark, outsized bags under each eye. I suspected that a fine white powder was involved. Stan would make a fine lounge rat someday. "That's too bad about her husband," I said, surprised. Here was some young guy with a family dying for my right to obtain blanket contracts from General Motors. I felt a tinge of guilt. Enough. Activism would have to wait.

Estelle delivered my cheeseburger and tab, smiled slightly and stood just far enough away with her hands on her hips to wait for other customers to come in. The band started playing an original and Stan faded back to the beer taps to listen. He was right; these guys were really good! The summer bock went perfectly with cooked beef and melted cheddar. While I ate quickly, five younger men came in and sat at the bar. Estelle skillfully exchanged tip-maximizing pleasantries with each of them (she talked to them more than she talked to me). I thought about her some more and wondered if she was related to Officer Munday. My tab was $12.32, so I left a twenty next to the plate and exited BO's without saying goodbye. Fine.

As I approached the bright aperture to the outdoors, Stan popped out and exclaimed, "Take care dude!" I looked over my left shoulder and waved to him like I was signaling a turn. I heard The Shy's song end and the crowd whistled and clapped for more.

It was still a nice day outside, and about a block south I saw a phone booth. While still searching my trousers for change (I do not recall why the MCI approach seemed too dangerous), I entered the booth and dialed a number that had not changed in thirty years, except for the area code.

My mother answered. "Hello?"

"Mom, it's me."

"Frankie?"

"Yes," I replied.

"Oh, how are you? Where are you?"

"Trying to figure out what's going on. How are you? And dad?"

"We're fine. Tell me what happened."

"I don't know yet. Tell me what's new with you two."

I heard her pull the phone away and tell my dad, Sam, to pick up the other line. "Well," she started,

"I finished that computer class at the community college, and I just got my AOL account started. I found a story about you on the net." Wait a minute, I thought; on the net?

"You're already on the internet? That is really great," I told her sincerely. Gladly, I never knew what to expect from them. It was good preparation. Neither one had ever used a PC until I showed them how to play solitaire on the infamous laptop a few weeks ago. The very next day she signed up for a weeklong continuing education class in 'Home Computer Use' at Macomb Community College. "What story did—"

"Hello?" Interrupted my dad.

"Hello?" I said.

"There you are, Sam," said my mom.

"Dad? It's me."

"You've been on the news."

"Sam! Stop it! Frankie, we know you didn't kill that British spy."

I froze. British what? "What do you mean, spy?"

"Like I tried to tell you, Frank," he continued, "you've been on the news and the net. The dead fella they think you mugged the other day was with the British secret service. There's an Officer Munday from Dearborn who keeps calling us, asking about you and your business. Of course, since you don't tell us anything we can't tell her anything. She thinks you had something to do with it though, that much I know."

I was paralyzed. "I have to go." I hung up the phone, stunned, but a little relieved that something was going on. There *was* some kind of conspiracy or cover-up! Once again I needed a taxi. Thank God for Cindy Salome's money. Look. Hail. Get in. Same routine.

"I need to go to the east side, Roseville," I told the unshaven driver, not fully understanding my need to go to the east suburbs of Detroit.

"Right away."

As the vehicle rolled south on Woodward, the main avenue connecting downtown Pontiac to Detroit's wealthy northwest suburbs, the driver, who was an average-looking Caucasian man with brown hair and brown eyes, spoke. "Do you mind if I listen to talk radio?"

"Nope."

"Great."

He tuned into the well-known, cigar-smoking radio host, Dirk Mott, who was very passionate.

"I'm Dirk Mott. Do you know who you are! Do you think the federal government is out of control? And how about the Defense Department and the IRS? And what about big business? How well do you think these leviathans know each other? Well, I am here to say: better than the average taxpayer will ever know! Do you even care? I submit that not enough Americans care enough about contributing to the future of America, that most of us only give a damn about a quick and easy buck, or a handout. Let the collectivist government handle it, we say. It enrages me to say collectivist, but that's what it is, people.

Have you forgotten that ours is a government for the people by the people? Take responsibility folks, or you'll be taken!"

"My next guest, A. Danby Heckman, has recently written a book called *The Lost Fortunes*, and in this book Mr. Heckman details how a wing of the Defense Department, the National Reconnaissance Office, NRO for short, has colluded with a still unknown group of retired automotive executives, who didn't really want to retire, to illegally launder and hide billions of tax dollars. Guess what? They can't find it! If you think I'm crazy, then stay tuned because there is a Detroit connection in all of this. Was a former General Motors executive murdered? Or did he die naturally, as his surviving son and daughter were told? We' get into this and more after a station break."

The driver and I were listening intently.

A commercial for home equity loans followed.

"What a diatribe," I said.

"Maybe, but he's right," the driver replied confidently. "I've read A. Danby Heckman's book." He looked me in the eyes through the rear-view mirror and held up the paperback in his right hand. "A few months ago, I once gave a taxi ride to the Detroit auto executive who was killed. He was very sociable and friendly."

"What auto executive?"

"Bennington. Arthur Bennington. It's all here in Heckman's book."

"The Arthur Bennington from General Motors?" I asked, stunned a second time in less than an hour.

"That's the one. Heckman claims that a retired executive from General Motors and corporate officers of Dickman Brothers Automotive, a Canadian mega supplier, were involved with hiding, and hiding, and hiding again, billions of tax dollars. According to Heckman, the NRO, a relatively small wing of the Defense Department, gets phony budgets approved and then drags its feet when it comes to spending specifics. They use the approved money from their phony budgets to work with executives like Bennington, and Larry Dickman, the chief financial officer for Dickman Brothers Automotive. Apparently... wait, here's Dirk Mott." He turned the radio up louder.

"Good afternoon, listeners. This is Dirk Mott, and today I have A. Danby Heckman with me to talk about his new book called *The Lost Fortunes*. Mr. Heckman —"

"Dirk, it's okay to call me Danby," Heckman interrupted.

"I can do that, Danby. So, tell us what you know."

"First, Dirk, I wish to thank you for having me on your show. America needs talk radio the way a judge needs honesty."

"I'm sure," replied Mott, "that several in Washington and at the Pentagon would disagree."

"Perhaps, but I am not here to give a damn what they think. I am here to share with Detroit the truth about the death of Arthur Bennington and his connection to Larry Dickman, a corporate officer for the Canadian automotive supplier of the same name. My book discusses a total of five retired GM execs gone bad, but only one, so far, has been killed. I speak of Arthur Bennington, a formerly successful, now dead man."

"Please, tell us about him."

"He was educated in engineering and business at Michigan in the fifties," began Heckman, "and privately felt proud of his Wolverine heritage. At times he expressed concern that too much of what was taught in the MBA and engineering schools at Michigan did not apply to the real world, but nonetheless spoke openly about how his education had served him well. Thus, he gave generously as an alumnus once he reached the executive role at GM. Bennington was the consummate company man and he rose steadily through the ranks of powertrain product design. He was part of the team that developed and patented the catalytic converter, which as we now know remains after twenty years the best way to minimize exhaust emissions. Following the successful launch of the converter in the late seventies, Mr. Bennington found himself in charge of GM's standards and regulatory division. He correctly considered this staff position, albeit executive level, a dead end career-wise. Bennington felt pigeonholed, or stuck, in emissions testing, and late in his career, after a solid fifteen years in the mundane vehicle certification business, he openly referred to himself as an executive compliance test engineer without a meaningful budget."

"Describe the significance of this, Danby," said Mott. "How about getting to the point?"

"I will Dirk, but this background is important. As it turned out, the branch of the NRO that recruited the DE's, or desperate executives, as referred to in several memos that we obtained by the Freedom of Information Act, got the idea to approach Bennington after they read an interview of him in Crains's *Automotive News* honoring Bennington's forced retirement. Although nobody at GM will verify this, his retirement was surely a result of Bennington's overt complaining within the company about poor testing practices. In the Crain's article, Bennington stressed how important it was to test thoroughly and not cut corners. He never came right out and said what specifically was bothering him, but subsequent research by my staff shows that he was cornered into providing test data which showed that two of the company's key vehicle lines satisfied federal requirements, when, in fact, they may not have. Bennington's test specialists developed a Taguchi test matrix that cost too much to complete. Now, for those listeners who don't know what a Taguchi matrix is, let me briefly explain a few things. When you buy a new car, you pick from a long list of available options like engine size, anti-lock brakes, wheel and tire size, and others. Believe it or not, these choices impact how well your new car will satisfy federal exhaust emissions requirements.

Consequently, the car companies must provide data to the government that shows that any available combination of options on a new car will still allow the vehicle to pass federal requirements. The problem is that mathematically there are several million possible combinations and nobody can predict exactly which ones people will buy. So, to properly test, a method developed by a Japanese scientist named Taguchi is used. This method uses a carefully selected number of option combinations to predict, beyond any reasonable doubt, the range of results for any possible option combination. I won't go into how this select group is determined, but think of a Taguchi matrix as a subgroup of vehicles that, when tested, can accurately predict how a so-called worst case vehicle will perform."

"That sounds like a very powerful engineering technique," Mott interjected.

"It really is?" Heckman continued, "Anyway, for two of GM's new vehicle lines, Bennington was unable to test even a streamlined Taguchi matrix of vehicles because of budget limits. And when he was pressed to prove it to his superiors, he relied strictly on the technical aspects of testing. Dirk, as you may or may not know, any competent emissions test engineer will tell you, the bean counters don't understand the technical side of things. And under pressure, Bennington proved to an engineer, which was his downfall. The only way he could see to obtain an acceptable comfort level was to perform more testing. The problem was that his own company would not allocate the necessary funding to have this work performed. Arthur Bennington started a huge internal political war at GM and lost. Coincidentally, soon after this, his retirement was announced. So in honor of his fine career and early work on the catalytic converter, *Automotive News* approached him for an interview to discuss Al Gore's position on automotive emissions. First, Bennington angrily explained that since Gore was a spoon-fed, thin-lipped politician with no profit margin responsibilities, he had little respect for his views, but unfortunately had to potentially abide by much of what he said. Bennington used the analogy of home inspectors that were failures as home builders and thus became home inspectors. It was them that he made the executive engineer without a meaningful budget statement. The NRO had always monitored these types of periodicals, and knew, and continues to know, that highly paid executives who are forced to retire rarely want to give up the action and excitement of a career. From this interview they recognized that Arthur Bennington might be willing to play in their arena. A few weeks after the Crain's article was published, about three years ago, the NRO covertly approached him."

"This is fascinating, Danby," said Mott. "Let's pick up here after a station break." The aggressive, angry theme song of Dirk Mott's program potted up, then faded out to make way for an advertisement for the Rush Limbaugh show, which was broadcast on the same station.

By then, we had driven enough south and were approaching I-696. I told the driver to take 1-696 east to Roseville. We passed the Detroit Zoo and then turned left onto the freeway.

After several minutes of commercials, Dirk Mott came back on. "Welcome back, listeners. We are here with A. Danby Heckman, author of *The Lost Fortunes*. Danby, pick it up where we left off."

"Thanks, Dirk. Well, it did not take the NRO long to seduce Bennington. Simply put, the NRO had made a deal with a certain high ranking general in the Cuban Army who was planning to overthrow Fidel Castro after the 1996 American presidential election. As you can imagine, such a general would be a welcome friend to the American military."

"Yes, Danby, I am well aware that our government agencies have illegal relationships with despots across the world! My friend, you are preaching to the choir."

"I know, sir," replied Heckman.

"Tell us about this deal."

"In return for his loyalty, this still unknown Cuban general would receive political backing after killing Castro and military equipment to make it happen. With the White House chock-full of liberal Democrats intent on slicing the military to ribbons, this was no easy task. In fact, a new level of creativity was required."

"As I recall from reading your book, this was where the automotive executives were needed."

"In effect, yes. Between 1900 and 1945, the world automotive business and the world military infrastructure were very closely connected. Ford Motor Company, Daimler-Benz, and others made billions from the World Wars. By 1970, fueled by the momentum of these profits, the American dream was alive and well, except for Vietnam and a few assassinations. The next two decades saw the rise of the more socially conscious governments, both here and in western Europe. Whether someone was simply lazy or truly in need made no difference; the government was there to redistribute wealth to whomever asked. At the same time, increases in taxation and in market regulations in areas such as food, drugs, communications, automotive, particularly exhaust emissions and mileage requirements, forced commercial companies to become very efficient and lean. But for military contractors, this did not happen until the Cold War ended in 1989. Since then, the American military-industrial complex has been reeling. I want to remind your listeners that I am not against regulations - when they are made by informed parties. The soon-to-be required zero emissions limits for automobiles sold in California are ridiculous! When Mount St. Helens erupted last decade, it spewed out orders of magnitude more pollutants than twenty years' worth of North American automotive exhaust."

"This is very interesting, wouldn't you say, listeners?" Mott said slowly.

"I found it disturbing, Dirk; that's why I wrote *The Lost Fortunes*. Not that it is right or wrong, but our military has been driven to extreme measures to protect our country's interests."

"Yes, the book title. What fortunes were lost?"

"I'll get to that, but let me first provide some more background."

"Fine. It's your book."

"Soon after Castro took over Cuba in 1959, American-owned companies were forbidden by executive order to continue operations there. Then, between the Bay of Pigs and the Cuban Missile Crisis, Cuba evolved into country-non-grata to the Americans. It was as if the great Caribbean Island simply disappeared like Atlantis. America's allies also basically avoided Cuba for the sixties, seventies, and eighties, right up until the Cold War ended in 1989. But since then, the American alliance against Cuba has slowly crumbled. In fact, our number one ally, Canada, has allowed several large Canadian companies to invest in and develop several Cuban markets: sporting goods, snack foods, commercial airlines, medical equipment, and the list goes on."

"There was a public television program about that recently, *Nova*, I think," interjected Mott.

"That's correct, Dirk. Bill Moyers did a piece three months ago. To my point, Dickman Brothers Automotive is a Canadian company with the freedom to do business in Cuba."

"Hold on, Danby," said Mott. "I thought that the state Department doesn't allow American corporations to do direct business with any foreign companies that deal with Cuba?"

"The key word is direct – direct business. General Motors purchases just under three billion dollars' worth of automotive components and systems from Dickman Brothers each and every year, yet GM cannot do business in Cuba. But, just over three years ago, GM lobbied to get a waiver for Dickman Brothers that would allow this key supplier to invest in Cuban property and capital on a case-by-case basis. It was approved by the Commerce Department, against the will of the State Department. Clearly then, GM executives are familiar with the manufacturing capabilities and high-level management practices of Dickman Brothers. Knowing this, the NRO asked Arthur Bennington to be a front for dealing with Dickman Brothers. You see, the NRO also knew that Mrs. Larry Dickman, the CFO's wife, and Mrs. Arthur Bennington were sisters. Over the years, the brothers-in-law Larry and Arthur had grown to be close personal friends."

"What did the NRO want with Dickman Brothers Automotive?" Asked Mott.

"Very simple: a world class, industrial manufacturing plant in Cuba that could be quickly modified to produce diesel powered, off-road military vehicles for an unidentified Cuban general. This general, in theory, could then use these vehicles to transport supplies from Guantanamo."

There were three or four seconds of dead radio air. "It all fits, Danby. But why not approach Dickman Brothers directly?"

"Too risky. The Dickmans had always been on the level, and the NRO could not risk that kind of international exposure. In Bennington, the NRO had a brilliant, innovative, and motivated executive who was a trusted friend of the CFO of Dickman Brothers Automotive. This, combined with Bennington's later, somewhat unstable years at GM, gave the NRO a perfect lackey if things went awry. The NRO could avoid direct dealings with a Canadian company, while maintaining the ability to simply deny any knowledge of Bennington. Besides, Arthur was forced to retire for some reason, wasn't he? Maybe he was losing it."

The two chuckled sarcastically.

"There must have been an agreed upon cut for Bennington and the Dickmans, then," said Dirk Mott.

"Yes. Five million dollars each per year, funneled to a Swiss account."

"That's not bad."

"Not bad at all. But what the NRO did not count on were the unknown dire straits of Dickman Brothers Automotive. This was compounded by the weak Canadian currency. One of the consequences of running lean, as any supplier to the big auto companies knows, is that the profit margin is always tight, and getting new business can be very difficult. At about the same time the NRO was working on Bennington, Dickman Brothers, in an effort to wrestle a large portion of GM's diesel engine business away from Detroit Diesel, had low-balled with a six hundred million dollar bid. Larry Dickman felt personally responsible for approving the bid, which was too low by over fifty percent. A three hundred million dollar shortfall, combined with a softening diesel market, can bankrupt even an eight billion dollar company."

"Is that US dollars or Canadian?" asked Mott.

"Good question. I mention in the preface of my book that all monetary quantities are based on the US dollar, as are those I just quoted."

"So, what went wrong?"

"Similar to the Ford family, just on a smaller scale, Larry and Henry inherited the company from their father, added 'Brothers' to the company name, and thus felt great pressure to recover from the diesel engine fiasco with GM. Wherever Larry Dickman was putting over a billion dollars from the NRO for the Cuban manufacturing facility, only he, his brother Henry, and Arthur Bennington knew. When it became obvious that five million per year for Henry and Larry was not enough to save their company, the brothers approached Arthur about keeping all of the NRO money and splitting it three ways. In other words, Bennington and the Dickman brothers intended to keep one hundred percent for themselves, and once they properly hid the funds in an off-shore account, they told the NRO to fuck themselves all the way to the bank."

"Whoa, Danby, this is not cable TV. I'm looking at an angry producer."

"Sorry, Dirk. I simply want your listeners to know the facts."

"Okay, my friend, but please try to give the facts without the fuck." You could hear Dirk and Danby laughing in the background. Talk radio was rolling!

Dirk called for a short commercial, and exit signs for Gratiot Avenue were immediately upon us. I remembered then about driving into the wall at Coolidge just a few days ago. I had not noticed the spot along the way; there was no evidence left on the great wall – none. I was no longer sure where it had occurred. Leaving a mark proved difficult.

"Get off at Gratiot and drop me over there at White Castle," I requested, pointing at the hamburger joint on the south-east corner of Gratiot and I-696.

"No problem." In the background – the driver had reduced the volume when I started giving directions since there was no way he could appreciate my focused interest in the story – I vaguely heard A. Danby Heckman continue with his story. The taxi pulled into the parking lot.

"That is sixteen dollars, please," the driver said.

"Fine," I replied. "If I give you forty dollars, will you give me your paperback book?"

His eyes focused in the rear-view mirror, happily puzzled.

"Sure," he said.

I gave him the money, climbed out, and reached for the book through the front passenger's window that had just opened.

Another marketing taxi driver, I thought, then walked towards the White Castle past two well-fed and unbathed Caucasian panhandlers who were hanging out in the parking lot.

"No," I told them before they asked. "I'm in worse shape than you?" Once inside I bought a large coffee and proceeded to confirm everything that the taxi radio had started to tell me by reading two hundred and fifteen pages in two hours.

I further learned that trust between the embezzling threesome disintegrated when Bennington's wife died from cancer the night President Clinton was re-elected. A. Danby Heckman had not fully uncovered the details, but apparently this drove Arthur Bennington to play his own game of hide-and-seek with the NRO money. He hoodwinked the Dickman brothers and the NRO, and kept it for himself.

By the time the NRO had, allegedly, decided to kill Bennington, he had approximately one billion illegal dollars to his name. He had angered everybody – his co-conspirators, as well as those involved at the NRO! Arthur Bennington managed singularly to stash away over a billion dollars that still has not been located. Not even his co-conspirators Larry and Henry know where the money is; they are under federal indictment and have been granted immunity if the money is returned.

The Senate Intelligence Committee, to which the NRO reports, is headed by Senator Arlen Spectator. Spectator has ordered the NRO to provide a full accounting of the Bennington billion, as it is now called in closed political circles, according to Heckman. It's one of those deals where everybody knows the NRO participated in the money laundering, killed Bennington, and maybe planned to kill others, but the proof, the money that is, can't be located. Consequently, so far, nothing has happened.

I regarded that Senator Spectator was the same man, acting then as a federal prosecutor from Pennsylvania, who developed, marketed, and sold the single-bullet theory of the JFK assassination to the Warren Commission. How could Spectator believe in any conspiracy if not that one? Even though the Senate Intelligence Committee had the wrong man in charge, he was my best hope - the man with the power. Maybe he knew what the false Seagate serial number meant. After all, it had ten digits in it, just like a bank account number. Talk radio had given me something to go after. I finished pondering and went to the bathroom in the castle, then left, telling the beggars that they wouldn't be young forever.

A phone booth was located at the edge of the parking lot. I entered, deposited, and dialed.

"Hello?" My mother answered.

"Mom, it's me again. Get a pencil and paper."

"Okay, Frankie, just a minute." A few seconds passed. "I've got them."

"Write this down."

"Okay."

"Senator Spectator, the location of the Bennington billion is related to the following ten-digit number: 1424679698. I know the person who knows where the number was hidden."

"Now what?" she asked.

"I need you to send this message to the senator from Pennsylvania on internet mail."

"What's this about, Frankie?"

"I can't go into it now, but I promise I'll explain. His e-mail address should be easy to find. Just send the message and I'll call back tomorrow."

"If you need me to do it I will. All right. I'm not worried, Frankie, AOL is anonymous, so they can't trace it to me physically, only virtually. Bye, honey."

She hung up, and I couldn't believe what I had heard. Only virtually?

CHAPTER EIGHT

There is no Earth.
This is all a mirage.
Life cannot be this complicated.
I have no other insight that I can see.

>Jerrold Edwin Brancaster

After hanging up, I dialed Cindy Salome at home. She usually left work early on Fridays, to prepare for the weekend. Ring, ring.

"Hello?"

"Hi, Cindy. It's Frank. Frank Drachman."

"Frank! You weirdo. How many Franks do you think I know? How are you? Where are you?"

"Right now, I'm on the phone and doing fine."

"I've been really worried about you." Pause.

"Thanks Cindy. But I'm doing better now that I am sure something is going on. What did you tell the police about the night Ian Hatley was mugged?"

"Wait. Rewind. I miss you, Frank."

"I miss you too, Cindy. Things are getting tight."

"I know. I told that Officer Munday that we went out for burgers at about eleven thirty."

"I don't take ginseng yet, but I do remember that I went alone and was gone for over an hour."

"I told Officer Munday what I told her."

"Well then, do you think I had anything to do with it?" I wanted to know.

"Not really."

"Not really?"

"You asked. I think you know more than you're telling me but I don't think you killed anyone."

"Cindy, wait a minute. I don't want to fight about anything with you, especially not this."

"Let's not then. Let me put it to you like this, Frank. We met three and a half months ago at a meeting. We went out two days later and then you told me you'd planned to file for a divorce, before we had met... I'm nervous... let me get my breath... you told me that your marriage to Beth the bitch was over. I don't even know how many times we've been together since, but it's mostly all I can think about. I filed for divorce too, and it will be final in five weeks! We've never talked about it in detail, but I know we were both thinking about cleaning out our closets and settling down whenever things were worked out."

"I never said Beth the bitch."

"What difference does it make? I've never felt this way about a man in my life! I know deep down you can't lie to me. I know from those nights that I am special to you. Either that or you are the world's greatest liar! If it weren't for Beth the bitch, and Harry, my no-good-lying-he-who-got-a-vasectomy-before-we-

were-married-and-didn't-tell-me-because-he-didn't-want-kids-piece-of-shit-soon-to-be-ex-husband, you and I wouldn't have been open to finding each other. Well, I've got news for you, Frank Drachman. We're cursed now because we found each other and I want to get married again and have a baby…"

She had worked herself into tears and I had just had both of my feet slammed back onto the ground. She was crying steadily in the background, the phone held away from her mouth but close to her ear, I suspected.

"Have you been taking your supplements?" I asked gently.

"What?" *Sob, sob.*

"Supplements. Vitamins."

"Don't ask me that now, Frank. I can't believe you." *Sob, sob.*

"Everything will be okay, honey," I tried.

"How in God's name do you know everything will be okay? Wait, don't answer me. I'll tell you how I've been able to sleep these past three nights: I love you more than I could have imagined possible. Marrying Harry Delrimple was simply a mistake. I can't explain it any better than to say I want to grow old and wrinkled with you... and I want to be surrounded with grandchildren on Christmas. So if I have to stretch the truth now about one night of hamburgers to keep that dream alive, I will. I don't care." She was weeping heavily.

I concluded that Cindy was hysterical and difficult to manage. "It's going to be okay, Cindy,"

I said, while quietly giving thanks that she did not adopt Harry's name in marriage. I was also concerned about her vision of me as an old, wrinkled grandfather. I still viewed myself as an up-and-coming test for profit engineer. But her conviction forced me to think more about how I felt about her. Being a fugitive was convenient on many fronts, and I needed to go. There were big mysteries to resolve!

"Frank," her voice crackled, "if it turns out that somehow you were involved with that guy's death, then it will come out and I can finally disregard any interests I have about men. I will be devastated enough and your going to jail or whatever happens won't phase me. Right now I am upset and angry and I miss you!"

Again, I did not know what to say. "Everything will be okay, Cindy. I love you. Don't worry so much." I tried them all.

"You really do?" she asked between hiccup-like gasps of air and tears.

"Really what?"

"Love me."

"Yes, Cindy, I do."

"Frank, I'm sorry I'm so PMS."

"It's okay, Cindy. Everything will be fine." We were both quiet and thoughtful for several minutes and I cried discretely away from the mouthpiece. I had no idea what had suddenly happened. Why was I upset?

"What are we going to do?" she, the consummate team player, asked.

I waited a moment before answering. "Well, I'm in town. Let's meet."

"You're in town?"

"Yes, but only for the day. The *day*." I hoped that she would figure out that I meant Friday's, home of the broken nose. She paused, then over the phone I heard her excitement and understanding.

"Frank, got it. Can't wait to see you. One hour. Bye."

I exited the phone booth. The sun was setting, and for a moment I remembered the nice texture of Cindy's look and the contrast of her dark hair against light smooth skin. I couldn't wait to see her. On top of it all, I still had several hundred dollars which afforded me the freedom to take a taxi cab all the way from Pontiac to Fairlane Mall in Dearborn, where the infamous Friday's was located.

A Pontiac cab was just coming out of the drive-thru at the White Castle, about one hundred feet away from me. I trotted over, book in hand, and asked if sixty dollars would get me to Dearborn.

"Sure," replied the attractive African American female driver, "if you pay first."

Trust, I thought, the key to the future. I complied emotionally, sort of mesmerized by her nice smell, paid, and climbed into the rear seat, wondering about her on-board cleaning arsenal. She was very beautiful, and I felt compelled to tell her that I did not want to talk during the ride, that the silence would not affect her tip. I wanted to know what she thought of me, but did not ask directly. For thirty-five minutes straight I explained how I simply needed things to be predictable and quiet, that A. Danby Heckman was an American hero and I needed to study his work. Hopefully she would understand and not put me in the same category as most. Finally, and most importantly, I explained that I was not usually this rude, but being a fugitive took its toll. All the while she effectively ignored my ravings, the ravings of a wanted test engineer. And she probably considered me a nutball. Just as I wanted, I imagined. Upon arrival at Friday's, I thanked her for her consideration and appreciable intellect.

As I exited babbling, she burst into laughter. "You are one nervous white boy. You go now and take care."

I realized at that moment that my skills with confidence and people were slowly crumbling. It was only a matter of time. I closed the cab door and walked into the bar, smiling at the young, door-holding buck who was thinking about the pretty hostess next to him. She asked if I was interested in a table or, "… will you be visiting our lounge area?"

"The lounge." All of the thirty or forty bar stools around the elevated bar area were occupied, so I overtly acted as though I wished to stand until one opened. One did and I sat down. Then an adjacent seat opened.

Then a cheerful bartender asked, "What'll ya have?"

"Do you serve beer here?" His enthusiasm irritated me.

"No sirree. We serve customers here!" He was just too happy, and on top of it he'd outdone me in wit.

I laughed. "This customer will have a Budweiser."

"Right away, sir."

It came quickly and I took it up with my right hand and swallowed a big gulp.

"Would you like something to eat with that beer?"

"No thanks. I'm waiting for someone."

"Right on, my good man. Call me as needed."

"Thanks," I replied. And that was the end of our quick exchange. I drank the beer amidst the smoky happy hour crowd and looked for Cindy Salome.

She arrived twenty minutes later. The best part about her entrance was how we honed in on each other immediately. She looked very lively and sexy, causing a throb.

She approached me smiling nervously and kissed me fully on the lips for several seconds. "Frank, seeing you is just what I've needed. How are you?"

I noticed her little crow's feet and kissed one. I smelled her pleasant, soapy scent and noticed a few gray hairs. "Fine. Do you want something? I know the bartender and have plenty of cash?"

"Ha, ha. A glass of white wine would be wonderful."

The bartender came over with raised eyebrows.

"White wine," I said. "Sauvignon Blanc."

He smiled in approval.

Then Cindy began, "Tell me what's going on with that computer. I'm really worried about you."

"All I know is that there's got to be some kind of information on it. Did you know the guy I bought it from was murdered?"

"No!"

"Yes, he was," I insisted.

"I didn't mean no as in no, he wasn't murdered. I meant it like, no, you're kidding. How do you know he was murdered?"

"It's all right here," I replied, pulling A. Danby Heckman's book from my rear pocket.

She looked marginally convinced; actually, skeptical.

"Did you hear about that on talk radio?"

"So what if I did?"

"Frank, those guys are nutty."

"Let's not go into it here, Cindy. Let's go somewhere private."

"All right. I'll drive." She smiled.

"I've got the drink tab covered." I, big shooter, left a twenty on the counter and turned around, and Cindy Salome was halfway through the door to the parking lot. I trotted to catch up. She was either angry or horny. We said very little during the thirty second drive to the Dearborn Hyatt, located within the Fairlane Mall complex. The mall was named after Henry Ford's nearby Fairlane Mansion. The man had owned Dearborn and still died, I mean, still did.

Together, Cindy and I entered the hotel and got a suite (for which I paid cash). During the ride on the otherwise empty elevator, we said nothing. I wondered what she had in her large overnight bag. We still did not talk. Once inside the room we agreed to shower, and I could not keep my eyes off those areas. Her too. Then she wanted to wash me. Then we kissed some and proceeded to the bed after rinsing and drying off. She was careful not to get her hair wet in the shower.

A half hour later the sheets were torn from three of four corners, and we were hungry and relaxed. Outside the sun was getting orange and on TV Peter Jennings was talking too much, subtly taking too much credit for what he did. Was I becoming a critic, of all things?

"Are you hungry?" she asked.

"Very."

We ordered cheeseburgers, fries, and salads from room service and ate everything. Between bites we talked about the night Ian Hatley was beat to shit. I realized again that Cindy genuinely wanted to be with me for a long time.

"Your alibi is rock solid, Frank. I'll bet I could pass a lie detector test! I know before I said not really on the phone, about you and Ian Hatley, but I know you didn't mug him or pay anyone to mug him. Remember *Bonfire of the Vanities?*"

"I saw the movie."

"Me too. And to me, the moral of the story was that a lie can be better than the truth sometimes."

Mars and Venus were never closer, except for Officer Munday, who suspected that Cindy might lie for me. But Officer Munday was somewhere between Mars and Venus, and I had to accept that she would not be receptive to any part of me. Officer Munday troubled me. How could I get her to share my opinion? A solution to that would have to wait, I thought.

"Did you read the book?" I asked.

"No. But in college I read his other supposed famous book."

"Which one?"

"Look Homeward Angel."

"What was that about?"

"I don't remember the details, but I didn't like it. A lot of those writers are not in touch with real life. Sometimes it's like reading the Bible – just too much work. I like Susan Minot's books. She tells a story like a poem."

"Who's she?"

"I don't know much about her. My sister gave me one of her books for my birthday." She came closer to my left side and put her left leg across my thighs…

Some hours later, I looked at the clock and saw it was 3.37 A.M. Cindy was sleeping soundly. I thought about my brother as a sack of bloody potatoes. I thought about the carjacker that died at the great wall. Fuck him. There was no way around it. Then I thought about the last time Mike and I played basketball. I beat him in one on one the day before we left Michigan Tech to go home for his last Christmas vacation. I thought about playing catch in a triangle twenty years ago. I thought about how much I wanted to talk to him. Then I thought about what a little person from Cindy and me would be like. Those thoughts over and over, and I fell asleep.

Cindy woke up at 7.30 and kissed me until I woke.

I kissed her back while she felt for it, but my mind was back onto figuring out who killed Ian Hatley.

"I loved last night," I said, while kissing her.

"Me too, Tarzan. I love you, Frank."

"Me too." I tickled her ribs.

"Stop it," she insisted weakly between giggles.

"Stop what? I don't know what you're talking about."

"Tickling…? laughing, giggling, happy, fake fighting back, me!"

"Oh, that. Okay, if you insist." We were both panting a bit from the physical effort.

"Do I have bad breath?" I asked.

"What? No. Do I?"

"Kind of," I lied.

"Why didn't you tell me?"

"I just did." Pause. "I'm kidding, Cindy. Your breath smells like flowers."

"Frank! I hate it when you tease me."

"I know." We both laughed and she pinched the inside of my thighs to get even.

"I give! I give!" I blurted between laughs. About ten minutes of quiet ensued. "Let's take a shower."

"Sounds great. I brought some underwear and jeans for you from my apartment. See?"

"Thanks! The skivvies I had been wearing were getting a little ripe."

"I know."

After showering and dressing, Cindy was curious. "What are you going to do? What's our plan?"

After ruling out fleeing to Canada or to Mexico, I was thinking very clearly. "I have no idea, really.

But my mom is connected to the internet so I plan on getting advice from Senator Spectator via e-mail."

"That's all?" Always asking the tough questions.

"I alone have to resolve this," I insisted, missing the obvious.

"Fine. What do you expect me to do then?"

"Give me a ride to my parents' neighborhood. You see, Cindy, the less you help me, the easier it will be to convince Officer Munday that you are telling the truth," I replied, somehow ignoring the severity of Cindy's forgone, accomplice-level help.

"Sure I will. Then what?"

"Do you still have that pager? Same number?"

"Yes."

"Keep it on, I'll contact you within a week. Watch the news too, because if I'm caught and indicted it will be a big story."

She looked queerly at me. We said nothing more and left the tussled room. The elevator was crowded so we kept quiet. Outside awaited a gorgeous Saturday morning – blue sky, slight breeze, a bit cool yet. Even the birds were happy. Cindy drove me to a phone booth in Harper Woods that was about three blocks from my parents' house. For general geographic information, review a AAA map of the metro Detroit area.

"I'll call you soon."

"You better."

"I will. Thanks for everything, Cindy. My clean underwear are great. I love you."

"Oh Frank... I'm so worried—"

"Everything will be fine." This time it worked. She gathered herself and smiled solemnly at me. I got out of the car and watched her drive away. I then entered the nearby phone booth and deposited two quarters and dialed.

"Hello?"

"Mom, it's Frank. Frank Drachman."

"Don't be silly, honey. I knew it was you before I answered."

"Well, did you get a response from Senator Spectator?"

"As a matter of fact, I did. Let me go upstairs to the computer room and open my mail box. These cordless phones are sure handy."

Computer room? That was the bedroom Michael and I shared as kids. I heard the *click click click* of her walking on the hardwood kitchen floor. Then about fifteen seconds later she sat down at the computer desk.

"Here we are…"

"What's dad up to?" I asked.

"He went to Sam's Club for toilet paper and chicken breasts."

"Oh."

"The reply from aspectator at usasenate dot gov reads, *Dear Sir or Ma'am, thank you for contacting the office of Senator Spectator of Pennsylvania. We are currently reviewing the information in your note. It would be very helpful if you could identify the person you referred to in your note. This could help the senator resolve any related issues. Thank you again for your interest in this matter. Best regards, Penelope Pierce, Assistant to the undersecretary of the office of Senator Spectator of Pennsylvania.* That's all it reads, Frank."

"They sure sound interested; don't you think?"

"Yes. Do you want me to tell them who you are? They might be able to help."

"No, no. Whatever you do, don't tell them. Have you noticed any black four-door sedans around the neighborhood?" I asked as one drove past the phone booth for the second time.

"No, not really. I could ask your father when he gets home."

"You should."

"By the way, how is the split-up with Beth going?"

"Don't ask."

"Just be careful that the new girl is really the right one before you have sex. And how about your car testing, how's that?"

"You remember Andy, right? Well, he's handling everything for now. I need to find out what those damn numbers mean. I can't be running from the law forever."

"I know. Your father and I have discussed it a million times. You need to figure out what happened to that British... Wait a minute, Frankie! Do you remember that million man march with the blacks in Washington?"

"Yes."

"Remember that Louis Farrakhan, who's supposed to be a minister of some kind?"

"Yes." I was becoming a critic and a yes-man.

"He gave a numerology speech that Rush Limbaugh replayed."

"And?"

"One of the things we did in computer class was surf the web, and Mr. Farrakhan's web site had an executable program for numerology that you could download for free. It's supposed to translate between coded numbers and letters. I downloaded it for my assignment and kept it, but never used it!"

I knew this was going nowhere but did not want to squander her enthusiasm. "Do you want to run the program with the numbers I gave you?"

"Why not?" she said. "Let me do a file search for... what was it called, *nasolve*, that's right." I heard her tapping the keyboard and clicking the mouse. "There it is... now I can run it from the Windows file menu..."

When Michael and I were boys, she used to talk her way through sequential tasks like that; making chocolate chip cookies (...I don't want to make the butter too soft...) or doing the laundry (...I don't want to wash bright colors in hot water...). I was her way of teaching us without our knowing.

"It's working Frankie! It's prompting for... well let me just read to you what the program is displaying."

"Okay," I replied.

"Enter N for numeric input data, A for alphabetic, or A N for both," she said.

"Numeric, N."

"N, return. Enter base number of data. Must be a positive integer between one and twenty-six."

"Base number?" I inquired, wondering a little more about the sophistication of Minister Farrakhan and this program. "Base ten, I guess."

"Let me enter that. Return. There. *Enter numeric data separated by spaces, with no number exceeding twenty-six*. Why is that, Frankie?"

"Twenty-six letters in the alphabet, I guess."

"Oh. Let me just enter the numbers you gave me before. One space four space two space four space." She continued through the ten digits. "Now I can hit return. There. Wow, this Pentium is fast. It's already done. It says alpha numeric code detected. Hit space bar to display results."

"What's the output?"

"Let me just hit the space bar. There are four lines of letters," she replied. "ADBDFGIFIH is the first. ADXFGIFIH is the second, NBDFGIFIH is the third. NXFGIFIH is the fourth. It looks like the program converted the numbers to letters. What good is that?"

"I'm not sure. I need to think about it. If everybody is after Bennington's billion, maybe it's in the National Bank of Detroit," I said, half-serious.

"Right Frank – NBD. That's where our account is. We go to the branch where Michael's girlfriend from high school works. You remember Michelle Brownley, don't you? She's married now to a nice fella named Richard Cartier. She hyphenated her last name."

"That's nice. Tell her I said hello. And tell dad too. I've got to go now."

"I will. Call us if you get arrested. We love you. Good…"

"Wait, one more thing. Could you do me a huge favor?" I interjected.

"Probably. What?"

"Could you surf the web for me?"

"Sure. I like doing it anyway. What are you looking for?"

"You know the big contract I got from General Motors? Well, some of the parts I tested and approved failed vehicle level prove-out testing. Could you do a chat room or website search for new GM large pickup truck owners and ask if anybody has had any kind of trouble with their brakes?"

"How new?"

"Six months or less." The vehicles with Bagelle ABS modules were launched for volume production and available to the public about five months ago. I wanted to find out if any truck owners had noticed trouble. It felt good to think about work.

"I'll look into it today. Take care of yourself, honey. Bye." *Click*. I hung up too. I think she was a little upset and saddened that her only living son was an outlaw.

I suddenly felt depleted. My mind started to race. Something was strange. As I exited the phone booth, four of those dark sedans screeched to a halt all around me. Several men in mirrored sunglasses leaped from them (about two per vehicle) and surrounded me. Only one held a gun, but all were wearing dark two-piece suits with a white shirt and dark tie.

The one with the gun spoke. "Mr. Drachman, we're from the Federal Bureau of Investigation. Your best chance for long term survival is to lie face down in your tracks and keep your hands away from your body."

I put my hands in the air. "What about my rights? What about Miranda? I listen to Dirk Mott," I argued.

He did not reply. They all moved closer.

I got on the ground.

Two of the non-speaking agents approached and frisked me and gave some kind of hand signal that meant I was clean. They stood me on my feet.

"Put your hands behind your back," said the armed leader.

I held my hands out in front of me.

"Behind your back, mister!" he said firmly.

"That's a double negative, officer. Behind my back means in front of me, if you use the back as the reference position. And since you didn't define..."

The two quiet agents firmly grabbed my arms (one each) and put them behind me. I was guided to an open car door.

I mumbled something about tax forms lacking clear direction, and felt a hand on my head.

The door closed and the leader came around and sat beside me. Then the two quiet, rough and tumble agents climbed into the front seat and the other cars sped off in different directions.

"Where are we going?" I asked. No answer. "My lawyer is Geoffrey Fieger." Still nothing. They didn't care. They were not about to say anything. I decided to think about those last six numbers. NBD then six numbers. What could it mean? Between thoughts and minor breakthroughs, I monitored our route and often told the driver to keep the fare under forty dollars. I suppose I was nervous. They were quiet.

"How about those Tigers? Bullpen is gonna kill 'em again this year. Do you guys play golf? Did you know that golf is an acronym for gentlemen only ladies forbidden? What kind of movies do you like?" No response. I concluded that Dale Carnegie needed another chapter in his book about how to get a G-man to talk; I was winning no friends nor influencing anybody. Then I asked, "Are we going to an airport?"

"Yes," answered the leader.

"Then where?"

"Washington DC."

"What for? Is there some clause in the Constitution that I missed?"

"It's for your own good, Mr. Drachman." I was surrounded by liberals! From his inner jacket pocket, he produced a silvery plastic ziplock bag. He removed a white cloth from the bag and covered my nose and mouth, forcefully. One of his hands was on my face, the other was on the back of my head. Handcuffed, I could not fight very well. And his gloved hands were very strong.

I became drowsy and passed out. That's all I remember.

CHAPTER NINE

> Thou hast known for generations that the best hope for contentment is to detach thyself from all expectations of contentment. Or, at least, thou should have known.
>
> Ben Trapt

Whatever it was that knocked me out also provided a splitting headache. No longer handcuffed, I was lying against a wall on a twin bed (a name that puzzled me since such a bed would never accommodate two people) covered with a white sheet in a gray room. The lights were in the ceiling and did not function well. The room had no windows. Still drowsy, I sat up and put my feet on the floor and reviewed. To my left there was a bathroom equipped with a toilet, shower, sink, toothbrush; all the things a person would need, except a razor. Against the wall opposite me there was a long wooden bench, and to the right was the door into the room. No pictures or windows or magazines. I half expected Rod Serling to walk in and explain what part of the twilight zone the past week represented. No such luck. Instead, I heard keys jingling, then the door unlocked, and in came the armed kidnapper and a tanned, well-dressed man in his sixties.

I did not get up. I felt Cindy's money in my pocket.
"How are you feeling?" The familiar one asked.
"Like crap."

"Mr. Drachman, I'm Senator Arlen Spectator. I've been looking forward to meeting you," the elder man said, extending his arm for a handshake.

I reciprocated. It had been over twenty-five years since I had shaken hands with someone highly ranked in government. When Mike and I were in grade school (near the end of my third grade) we won a community service award for saving a swan with a broken wing. It was in the morning and we missed the bus. Not wanting to risk the associated repercussions of playing tag on the way to the bus stop, we decided to walk to school. It made no difference to the penal system there if we were five minutes or thirty-five minutes late. Anyway, we saw a swan lying with a funny looking wing in a ditch near the school, Canal Elementary, and so I gave it my peanut butter (no jelly) sandwich. I thought it was going to choke to death on the peanut butter. I told Mike to run in and tell my third grade teacher, Mrs. Washer. He did that while I apologized to the swan and hoped it didn't die. It couldn't even quack. Mrs. Washer called the city dog catcher, and twenty minutes later the swan was in a veterinarian's office being fixed.

At the start of the Memorial Day parade a few weeks later, we received a big blue ribbon with

'Community Service Award' written on it and we got to shake hands with the mayor. It was a fine day. The next year my parents transferred Michael and me to a Catholic school named St. Raphael's. It was here that I inquired about nuns and titles. It is unlikely that the swan and the transfer were related. Back to the gray room and the senator.

"How come?" I asked. "What in God's name is going on?"

"Not so fast," interjected the lead kidnapper, "you are in no position to..."

"It's all right, Mike," interrupted the senator, commenting first, then looking at me. "Agent Philips here is simply following orders."

"So, your name is Mike Philips then," I said. "Why was that such a secret back in Michigan?"

He didn't respond, but the senator continued. "I am very sorry that this has caused you so much trouble." Pause.

You should be, I thought.

"On the other hand, the Dearborn Police, particularly an Officer Munday — that's correct isn't it, Mike?"

'Yes."

"An Officer Munday is convinced that you killed Ian Hatley. I think you and I can help each other."

"How?" I asked.

"Agent Philips has told me that you have read A. Danby Heckman's book. Is that correct?"

"Yes. Cover to cover."

"At White Castle?" asked the senator, clearly in full knowledge of the answer.

"How long have you guys been following me?"

The senator looked at the agent, who pulled out a Columbo-like pocket spiral notebook, flipped a few pages, and, sounding bored, explained. "We had the Detroit office put out a bulletin on you the day Ian Hatley died. Although we don't always see eye to eye with the Brits, when it comes to dead agents, we try to cooperate. 'Frank Drachman' were his last words. As you must understand, we had to investigate. The first step was to complete a thorough background check on you and your accomplice, Cindy Salome."

"She's not my accomplice. I'm responsible for all this. Both of you better understand right now that Cindy and my parents remain untouched by anything, or I will not cooperate," I said, imagining hearings and depositions and tax audits.

"Untouched?" Agent Philips asked. I sensed sarcasm.

"Untouched." I replied.

"Untouched?" Inquired the senator. I sensed stupidity.

"Untouched! What part of untouched don't you guys understand?"

They looked at each other. "That may be more difficult than you think," began Agent Philips, "unless, of course, we find the Bennington billion."

Fuck you, prick-face, I thought while blocking my anger. "What else do you need from me?" I said flatly.

They looked at each other again. I was beginning to think they had a thing for each other.

"Just answers to a few questions," Philips said. "First, have you had any formal training in espionage? Our records don't show any."

"No. What records?"

"Just the case files. That is surprising, however, considering how you effectively eluded two worldclass operatives."

I wanted to blurt out, I just read books like Robert Redford in *Three Days of the Condor*, but did not. Instead, I asked, "What operatives?"

Agent Philips looked at Senator Spectator (see what I mean?) for guidance on what to say next.

His head nodded affirmatively and the agent spoke volumes.

"When you returned from a business trip to Arizona shortly after the death of Ian Hatley you were carjacked at the Detroit Metro Airport. We know that the man who died when you crashed into the wall on I-696 four days ago was a crude, violent former East German mercenary named Gunter Legglar. The late Mr. Legglar was often hired by the Cuban military to find and return or destroy, shall we say, prized information. We are reasonably convinced that when done with his inquisition of you, he was going to kill you."

"I know that," I said. "And by the way, except for reading a few Tom Wolfe books, I have had no formal training in spying. I simply want to go home again to my old life." We all paused together. A real team effort. I continued. "You said there were two operatives."

"Yes," said Agent Philips. "Just yesterday we confirmed with the CIA that you somehow eluded one of their top undercover shadows, Martin Tate. That's his name for this month anyway. Evidently—"

"Wait, wait a minute," I interrupted, while the senator watched. "Why are you telling me this?"

They looked at each other again! The agent spoke. "We are after the truth. You have no record. We need to trust one another."

I pondered his explanation.

He continued. "The CIA was on to you about thirty-six hours before the FBI, and they put a shadow on you right away. Then, out of nowhere, Agent Tate showed up at the Cincinnati Federal Building with scraped hands and knees and a very sore neck. He was quite angry according to what we've been told."

I felt a private sense of victory. "That's tough bananas for Tate. He's about five six, right? He followed me back from Arizona. He's not such a great shadow."

"Either that, or you are not just a test engineer," said Agent Philips.

"Do you understand now how far-reaching your situation is?" Asked the senator. "You must consider that two American government agencies, the CIA and FBI, and two foreign government agencies, the British secret service and, we believe, the Cuban military, are trying to get something from you. Had we not intercepted your phone conversations and brought you in, I'm not sure you'd be alive right now."

"What day is it?" I asked.

"Sunday," they said together.

Cindy's period was almost a week late, I thought. "What time is it?"

"Noon," said the agent.

"Are you both democrats?"

"Yes," said one.

"Yes. I was elected as a democrat," said the other. "Why do you ask?"

I was just curious, but felt a direct response was required. "Just curious," I replied.

They looked at each other. We all just sat quietly paused, like in group therapy when that last group member finally learns that silence is acceptable. I went into group therapy for a while after Mike died and there was this one fucking dickwad who couldn't shut up. When he finally learned to, I quit. What a self-oriented dickwad. I wondered if my life was falling apart again.

"So, gentlemen," I said to break the silence, "what's next?"

"Tell us what you know about the Bennington billion," began the senator. "You have read A. Danby Heckman's book. You purchased Arthur Bennington's computer. You are a very bright man, Mr. Drachman. You tell us what's next."

"Where are your sunglasses?" I just felt like it.

"What?" Said one.

"What?" Said the other.

"Never mind. Everything I read in Heckman's book rings true to me."

"Be careful what you read," cautioned the agent.

"What Agent Philips means, Mr. Drachman, is that Mr. Heckman has compiled a great deal of information from anonymous sources that is consistent with the findings of the Senate Intelligence Committee, the entity to which Agent Philips reports."

"I thought the legislative and executive branches were separate."

"Which brings me to an important point," said the agent quickly. "We discovered a slip of paper in your pocket with some numbers written on it. These are the same numbers that your mother sent to Senator Spectator's office. What do they mean?"

"What do you mean what do they mean?" I asked.

"I mean, what do they mean?" Countered the agent.

"I know you mean that you want to know what the numbers mean, but that doesn't mean..."

"Hold on!" interrupted the senator firmly.

"Just being near you federal types makes things more complicated," I added.

The senator slowly shook his head, then spoke deliberately, suddenly producing a familiar slip of paper from his jacket breast pocket. "I will ask this one time with no strings attached. Do these numbers mean anything to you with respect to the Bennington billion?"

"Other than the fact that I found them on Arthur Bennington's Seagate hard drive, no, they don't." I noticed Agent Philips taking mental notes. We all said nothing for a few seconds. I thought of Dale Carnegie. Had I blundered in offering this information? It felt like group therapy. I had to speak.

"I've told you both everything I know," I lied. "And furthermore, I want to get back to Michigan and get my name cleared. There is a particular police officer I want to get off my back, too." The confusion surrounding the previous week of my life was clearing up. However, there were a few details on which I needed closure.

"I have two of my people clearing your record with the Dearborn Police Department as we speak," said the agent. There's just one thing I don't understand: why did you punch that British agent in the nose at the Ford Design Center? You had never even met him."

"That's incorrect, Agent Philips. Like I told Detective Carmichael and Officer Munday: Ian Hatley assaulted me a few months ago at a Dearborn restaurant."

"So, you're standing by that story then?" Asked the senator.

"Yes, I am. It's the truth."

"What would you say if I told you that I could prove without doubt that your story was false?" Replied the senator.

My butt hole tightened up. "What do you mean?" I asked.

"We've done a rigorous check with the Brits," began Agent Philips, "and the timeline you give for your encounter with Hatley cannot be true. Until three weeks ago, he had been on assignment in Kenya for the previous six months. There is no doubt about this, Mr. Drachman."

It tightened more. I could not speak. No shit, I thought.

He continued. "There is just no way Hatley could have broken your nose. Is it possible that the man who assaulted you and Ian Hatley were not the same person?"

"That's a very good question, but why would a British agent be following me around the Ford Design Center?"

"That is a particular detail we are still trying to nail down," said Senator Spectator. "It appears to be related to a diesel engine factory located a few miles outside of Nairobi. Evidently, plans to expand and upgrade this factory were suddenly scrapped last November, and the Kenyan government was very angry, claiming that the British government's lobbying for a Canadian diesel engine manufacturer was done in bad faith."

I recalled that the Queen of England still shows up on Canadian money. "Are you saying that Dickman Brothers Automotive scrapped an expansion plan in Kenya to build a new plant somewhere else?" I asked, knowing full well that this had to be the connection and that Cuba was the somewhere else.

"Mr. Drachman, we may never be able to prove it, but what you just said makes a great deal of sense. I'd bet that A. Danby Heckman will provide more information in his follow-up book about the Bennington billion." Replied Agent Philips.

The senator nodded in agreement.

It all fit together, except for the numbers on Bennington's hard drive. What did they mean?

"So, what do you and the government code breakers think the numbers mean?"

"I can only say that we are still trying to identify the potential encoding schemes that Mr. Bennington may have used," answered Agent Philips, after, naturally, eye contact with Senator Spectator.

"Okay then, how do I get back to Michigan?"

"The same way you got here. Blindly," replied the agent.

"We don't want to drug you, so please cooperate." He pulled a black hood from his inner jacket pocket. The same pocket as before.

Then the senator spoke. "Mr. Drachman, I apologize for any inconvenience we may have caused you, but until my subcommittee resolves the mystery surrounding the Bennington billion, I have asked Agent Philips to handle this and any related situation with the utmost security. It really is in your best interest for us to keep you in the dark until things are resolved."

"Huh," I replied as a statement not a question, while internally questioning their roles as civil servants. Who was serving who? I concluded that he actually meant that I did not know what was best for me. He was probably correct, but maybe not. "Let's get it over with then."

Agent Philips handed me the hood to put on my head.

I regarded him skeptically, then complied. The now black room was quiet. I noticed the senator's expensive (assumption) cologne and felt a need to comment.

"I didn't know Sears had their own line of cologne."

"Excuse me?" Asked the fine-smelling servant. I am sure they looked at each other.

"Never mind. It's enough for me to know that I'm helping two civil servants such as yourselves." Agent Philips sensed my intended sarcasm.

Senator Spectator did not; he believed me.

Agent Philips gave me a pat on the shoulder to get up. I did, then said, "Before I go, I have to go." They both sighed.

"Okay," said one of them.

I pulled the hood back and entered the toilet room, unzipped, urinated, shook, zipped, washed, dried, and pulled the hood down. It was very likely with these two that if push came to shove, I would be on the losing end of a frame-up conspiracy. The senator and his cohort would most certainly deny the past several hours, for my own good, of course. I was led out the door behind the senator (the smell gave him away) and in front of the agent. Soon after, two other agents I could not see or smell gently but firmly accosted me and we all proceeded through several turns and doors. It felt like a date.

Then, bang, we were outside, surrounded by helicopter blades loudly pushing sound waves traveling one thousand feet per second. Naturally, being hooded at the time, this is conjecture.

Nonetheless, I further concluded that I was somewhere in Virginia against my will, near some taxpayer-funded government building. For the people by the people? I heard the helicopter take off. It was probably the senator since I no longer smelled him. Then I was guided onto a small, comfortable aircraft (assumption, later confirmed).

Agent Philips made his presence known.

The small jet taxied and took off.

Still hooded, I pretended to look out the window as a sign of protest. Several quiet minutes passed.

"Beautiful view from up here," I said. No answer. No comments. "This is bullshit. Less government is better. You are all overpaid. You are dolts," I goaded. Still nothing from any of them. The ride was smooth and shortly we leveled off. I smelled a woman's perfume.

"Would you like something to drink, Mr. Drachman?" She inquired.

"Very funny. How am I supposed to drink it with this hood?"

"We're high enough to remove that," said Agent Philips. There was a pause.

I heard movement, then felt the gentle working of her hands. The hood came off and she brushed the hair out of my eyes. "How's that?"

"Better. Thanks," I told her, blinking the darkness out of my eyes. I was in the aft area of a new Gulfstream jet, surrounded by Agent Philips and a pleasant, heavy woman. She was wearing a blonde wig and sunglasses. Good disguise. It's no wonder great concern exists for the American intelligence community.

"Thank you," Agent Philips said to her.

"Mike, can I buy you a drink?" I asked.

He looked at me and smiled arrogantly.

I was gushing with excitement and relief because my name was cleared and I could again confront Officer Munday and Detective Carmichael. And I could even call my lawyer, Ben David Fisher, and Brook Taberman, the intern from Ben's office that I carjacked, and apologize. My innocence was fully backed by federal law.

"Don't you ever get tired?" He asked.

"Mike and I will both have a Rob Roy, with Dewar's and a cherry," I said.

The heavy woman checked with Agent Philips and he nodded yes.

"I'll return in a moment," she said.

Then Agent Philips stood up from the seat directly across from me and followed her, saying nothing.

I was alone, sitting in one of four saddle bucket seats (two facing two) surrounding a secured, wooden table. There were small floor mats in front of each bucket seat. Each of the seat backs had nickel-sized leather covered buttons in the center. I pulled a four inch long strand of straight brown hair from the top of my head and started a fish hook knot. I turned to my right and looped the hair around the adjacent seat's button, then pulled such that the knot tightened around the underside of the button and disappeared, perfectly. I pried up one side of the button and broke off the remaining two-inch pigtail, leaving only a small ring of my hair completely hidden under the button. I put the leftover piece of hair under the floor mat on which my feet rested.

A few minutes passed. She came back and set down two drinks on the table and stood quietly for reasons I still do not understand.

Agent Philips came right after that and sat directly across from me. He had removed his usual hand wear, and it was the only time, before or since, that I ever saw him not wearing leather gloves.

I drank first.

He followed.

"Thanks. A fine mix," I commented on the drink. "How will I know if the Dearborn Police have taken me off their list?"

"Call them." He extended a cell phone across the table.

"Now?"

"Sure. Hit the recall button. I just spoke to Detective Carmichael and told him you'd be calling."

I turned on the phone and pressed the RCL button. *Ring ring*. Then *ring ring ring*.

"Dearborn Police, Officer Ayoub."

"Is Detective Carmichael in?"

"Is this Mr. Frank Drachman?"

"Yes."

"Hold on." About ten seconds passed.

"This is Carmichael. *Bouuupp*. Whew, excuse me. I just ate
some tomato kibbee."

"Still noisy I see."

"This must be Frank Drachman. A man no longer wanted by my office."

"This is Frank Drachman. I understand that the FBI has clarified my innocence for you and Officer Munday?"

"That's correct, Mr. Drachman."

"So that's it?"

"Yes."

"How's Officer Munday?"

"*Bouuupp*. Excuse me. You don't want to know, Mr. Drachman. Officer Munday does not like you in the least."

"Why not?"

"God only knows. She likes everybody." I was hurt. "Huh. Tell her I said hello."

"Will do." We both were quiet except for his labored breathing into the phone mouthpiece.

"Bye."

"Goodbye, Mr. Drachman. *Bouuupp*, damn kibbee gives me hot pipes..." *Click*. I closed the phone and returned it to Agent Philips, then took a large gulp of my drink.

He sipped his drink.

"So that's it?"

"Legally, you are in the clear," he said.

There had to be a catch. "What does that mean?"

"It is a clear statement. Think about all the elements of your life: law, marriage, family, friends, business. Did I miss any?" His tone became more arrogant and vicious.

"Yes. Does Ed Finninen work for or with you? Was he sent to seduce my wife? Why didn't you just break into the house when nobody was home?" My question answered itself. They tried that and found nothing!

Agent Philips was listening and thinking. "You're supposed to be a smart man, Mr. Drachman, or am I mistaken? What do you think? Do you believe in coincidences? I don't."

"I may not know everything... but nothing had better happen to my parents or Cindy or Wil or Beth or Andy." I was angry and at a loss for words. Free advice for federal agents: never challenge an angry test engineer.

"You are not in any position to threaten, Mr. Drachman. You and your smart-aleck approach to life. Do you think we don't know about your score of eight hundred out of eight hundred on the quantitative part of the GRE exam? You didn't go to graduate school; we know that too. So what? So what if you turned down an invitation to join Mensa. You are as good with numbers as any world-class mathematician. I think you know one hell of a lot more about those numbers than you say. The vice will tighten. One billion dollars is a lot of money. You might soon find that General Motors has reviewed the blanket contract they recently awarded Forward Research and Test and concluded that your company is too unstable and risky, shall we say, to invest in."

"What the fuck is going on?"

"You tell me, Mr. Drachman. There are several influential operatives in your corporate neighborhood."

"I thought GRE scores were confidential," I said, ignoring his idle threats.

"They are," he replied.

I was fully confident. Perhaps his insults brought him down a peg. I couldn't put my finger on it. I reached for my drink and intentionally knocked his glass over. It spilled onto his shoes.

"God damn it," he said. "Can't you watch what you're doing! I'll be right back. These shoes are brand new." He left.

I swapped glasses without touching the outside of his glass. Since mine was nearly empty, he wouldn't know the difference. I wrapped his glass in a dry napkin and held it from the bottom, pretending it was my drink.

He came back after a while and sat down.

"Are you a communist, Mike?"

"Following orders. I can only help you if you are frank with me about what those numbers mean."

"That's my name."

"What?"

"Never mind. I have no idea what those numbers mean." I lied. In fact, I had countless theories, and to be honest, a billion laundered dollars was not a bad thing to have. "Did I just hear you say that you are going to somehow cause me to lose my GM blanket contract?"

The small jet began to descend. "Buckle up, Mr. Drachman. A seat belt could save your life again." I thought about trying to beat the shit out of Agent Philips. *Mano 'y mano*. But I knew he could beat the shit and the stuffing out of me. Control your anger. Think. *Comprendo 'y comprendo*. Think.

"This is bullshit, Agent Philips."

"No, Mr. Drachman. This is reality." Several minutes later, the plane landed at Flint's Bishop Airport. We unbuckled, but stayed seated.

Agent Philips gave me a hundred dollars cash, five twenties thumbed off of an appreciable roll, during the final taxi to a remote terminal. The jet stopped and the turbines wound to a halt. We stood. He escorted me to the exit door.

I kept the drink. "I'm not done. Can I take it with me?"

"Fine," he said after an irritated pause. "A shuttle will drive you to the main terminal. You can take a Metro car back to your apartment. One hundred dollars will cover it." Since I still had several of Cindy's twenties, I was not worried. I rolled up the money from Agent Philips, careful not to touch the middle three bills. The exit door swung open.

"Sure glad to assist you civil servants," I said to no one in particular. I walked down the stairs to the tarmac and climbed aboard the shuttle. During the short ride to the domestic terminal, I finished the drink, careful not to touch the glass with my fingers. I thought of his fingerprints on the money and glass. The agent had blundered.

CHAPTER TEN

Regardless of whether or not you are driven by capitalism or collectivism, or some combination of both, a successful life is directly related to your perception of hope and rubble.

W. Stewart Drost

I stood in the bland domestic terminal of Bishop Airport, filled with hope for the future. There were only a few people in the airport and I had to think to recall what day it was. Sunday. It was Sunday, and I did not feel much like riding in a taxi for an hour and a half back to my empty apartment in Novi. I had had enough of that. I looked around for a payphone, found one, then placed a call, a collect call, to Cindy Salome. Zero, then the area code and number, which will not be reproduced here for security purposes.

"A T and T. How may I help you?" Said a mild, male voice.

"Collect call from Frank W. Drachman." I don't know why I included my middle initial.

"Placing the call now, sir?" *Ring. Ring.*

I heard Cindy answer. "Hello?"

"Will you accept a collect call from Frank W. Drachman?"

"Yes. I will."

"Thank you for using A T and T."

"Hello?" I said.

"Frank! How are you? Where are you?"

"Cindy, it's me. God am I glad you were home. I know I said I'd page you, but I have no change. Just bills." There was a brief, quiet pause. I'd puzzled her.

"Don't be crazy. I don't care about that," she replied. "Where are you?"

"I'm in Flint. Cindy, I was drugged and kidnapped by federal agents and flown to Washington on a private FBI jet for questioning!"

She said nothing, which indicated concern. "Have you been drinking?"

"No. Well, I had a Rob Roy with an FBI agent on the return flight, but I'm not drunk. I took his glass. Ha!" I heard growing excitement in my own voice. I looked at the glass in my left hand and held it tightly.

"Oh no," she said. "This thing has pushed you over the edge. Where are you really?"

"Flint, like I said. Can you come and get me?"

"Yes, of course. How do I get there?"

"Simple. Take I-75 north to I-69 west and follow the signs to the Bishop Airport domestic terminal?" I paused, then continued.

"Cindy?"

"What?"

"I'm off the hook! I answered questions in Washington and then called the Dearborn Police from the FBI jet. My arrest warrant for the murder of Ian Hatley has been dropped!" I was in a lather of excitement.

"Okay, Frank. Just stay calm and I'll get there as soon as I can. How long will it take from my apartment?"

"An hour or so," I figured aloud. Even though Cindy was concerned for my sanity, it was reassuring to know that she still trusted my knowledge of basic physics (time equals distance divided speed) and directions.

"That's not bad. I'll see you in an hour. Bye."

"Bye."

Click. She hung up first.

I felt like celebrating my new freedom! Right next to the payphone, there was an open lounge with free pretzels. I walked over and sat down at the bar. A woman in her fifties approached.

"Are these pretzels free?" I inquired.

"If you buy a drink," she replied, obviously not amused. Perhaps Agent Philips was right about me. Nah, "Huh," I stated. Five or maybe ten seconds of quiet ensued. She looked at me with a stern but polite expression.

"Do you want something to drink?"

"Me?" I was pushing it.

"I ain't talkin' to your guardian angel."

"Well, then, I'll have Rob Roy. With Dewar's and a cherry."

"For two more bucks you can make it a double."

"Make it a double then. But before you do, could you please get me a clean paper towel and a bag? I have to store this glass safely."

"Sure. Whatever you say." She went and came back with supplies. I wrapped the glass and put it in the brown paper lunch bag she brought. I sipped my double. Before the hour expired, I had a few more doubles. And not enough pretzels. My perception was hazy as she approached blowing cigarette smoke from her nose like a dragon.

"Another?"

"No thanks. About how long have I been here?"

"You sat down at, let me see here, six fifty-four," she replied after looking at the date time on my bar bill.

"That's darn observant of you. You ought to be a private eye," I told her. She smiled sadly. I had been drinking Rob Roys and eating pretzels for an hour and ten minutes. It was time to go.

"I ought to be a lot of things kiddo. Are you set?"

"Yes. How much?"

"Twenty-two."

I gave her two twenties. "Keep the change." I was somewhat boiled and my thoughts paralleled. Perhaps it was the fourth double. I got up and walked toward the automatic doors. Technology, I thought. Nothing to worship. It can't change all the boundaries, only the lesser ones. Outside, I must have been wobbly as I stood waiting, not noticing the weather, waiting for Cindy Salome. Then, presto, her little car appeared.

The passenger door was unlocked and I opened it and climbed in. I sort of lost my balance and hit my head hard, then sat back. I immediately felt her cool hands on my warm, red cheeks and her lips on my lips.

She smelled nice and kissed even better. She put her arms around my neck and I reciprocated.

Something needed to be said, however.

"I'm off the hook! A protected species!"

"What? You smell like alcohol," she said while pulling away from me just a little.

"Hug me, flower petal," I said. "It's Rob's fault."

"What is? Is Rob the secret agent on the plane?"

"No. no honey. Rob Roy – Scotch and vermouth with a bing cherry."

"And who in the world flower petal? Is that what you used to call Beth? You're drunk. Let's not talk."

Oops. Confronted, I had only one alternative. Deflect, "Like you never called Harry Delrimple, Tarzan!" I retorted, trying to sound angry. But I really wasn't. But flower petal was angry. She rolled her eyes and turned up the radio. I was no match for her. I put my head back and fell asleep. Sometime later…

"Frank. Frank, wake. We're home."

The sun was setting and I recognized her apartment building. I felt dizzy and nauseous and stoned.

Cindy unbuckled my seat belt and got out. She walked around the car and opened the passenger door.

"I've got some of your money left over," I offered.

"Come on, Frank Drachman. You need to go to bed." Flower petal had calmed down.

"Let's go out and celebrate."

"You're something else," she said, half-chuckling out of frustration. "You need to go to bed. Come on."

I knew she was right. Tomorrow was Monday and we both had to get back to work. More importantly, I had to call Burt Morgan at GM and ask about my potentially retracted blanket contract. And if so, why?

Cindy and I trudged up the stairs to her third floor, one bedroom apartment. She fumbled with her keys then unlocked the door and we went in. I felt nauseous and stumbled to the bathroom. I did not vomit and ten minutes later I exited the bathroom.

She was sitting on the floor against the wall outside the bathroom. "Are you sick?"

"Almost."

"Did you eat dinner? Are you hungry?"

"No. Yes," I replied after considering the order of her questions.

"I'm warming up some homemade chicken noodle soup."

"Great. That's sounds really great. Do you have any Gatorade?"

"I sure do. Come in the kitchen. Let's eat. I'm hungry too. I've been working all afternoon to prepare for my meeting tomorrow."

I was exhausted and on the downside of too much Scotch, and was not talkative. Cindy was preoccupied with her meeting preparations. We ate the soup quietly and I drank two half liter bottles of lemon lime Gatorade. Cindy drank water with her soup. After, I offered to clean up the kitchen so she could get back to her work and she accepted.

"Thank you. I have a lot to read."

Then I said, "But I think I should go to my apartment tonight and check it out. The last time I was there, it was surrounded by police cars from Novi and Dearborn."

"I can take you over there, Frank, but I drove by yesterday and everything was fine. I even went inside. It looked okay to me. Why don't you just stay here tonight?"

Since I really didn't want to go to my apartment, I was quickly convinced by Cindy's description. It could wait until tomorrow. "Thanks. I really just want to take a shower and go to bed."

"Good. I've got an early day tomorrow." I stood up from the table and kissed her on the lips.

She kissed back. When we stopped, she went to the bedroom and I finished the dishes. Then I headed for the shower.

After carefully removing the money from the pocket, I put my clothes in her hamper, showered and dried. I wrapped myself in the towel she left out and went into the bedroom, money in hand. The bed covers were pulled back and Cindy was lying, legs crossed at the ankles, on the sheets in light blue underpants and a plain white T-shirt. Nothing else. She was reading a book and looked extremely good.

"Don't you look nice," I told her.

She looked up and smiled. "Thanks."

"Did you bring in the bag I had with me?"

"Yes, it's there on the dresser"

"What are you reading?" I asked.

"*Beyond Re-Engineering*." She showed me the cover of the book. I have to make a presentation tomorrow to three vice presidents about how Ford 2000 helps in the harmonization of international standards, now that Ford is re-engineered. Exciting stuff, don't you think?"

"Well, as you know," I began sarcastically, "standardized testing is the life blood of Forward Research and Test. Absolutely nothing else matters!"

She had already started to laugh at my fake intensity, which was particularly absurd since I was wrapped in a towel.

Then I told her, "It's smart to do your homework."

"I know."

"I shan't distract you anymore, Miss Salome. I shall brush my teeth and go to bed whilst you do your homework." I put the money in the bag with the glass. "Don't move this."

"You're so weird," she said in a good way.

I went to the bathroom and the steam on the mirror was gone. I looked terrible - just terrible! Nonetheless, I brushed my teeth and hair and hung up the towel and returned to her room fresh-breathed (reasonably) and naked, and climbed in and covered up.

"Goodnight," I told her. I leaned over and kissed her there through the T-shirt.

"Sleep tight." She smiled but was, understandably, engulfed in the book. Those fifteen minute presentations to executive management are career makers, or breakers. And Cindy had every intention of making it until something or someone more definite came around.

"It started today, Frank."

"What did?" I asked.

She put the book down and looked at me. "My period."

"Oh." I forgot that I was supposed to be relieved.

"I still want to hear about the secret agent and the private jet too."

I couldn't tell if she was serious and I reflected that for being such a smart-ass myself, I was not very good at perceiving others' mind games.

"There's really nothing more to tell," I said seriously. "But I am worried that the GM blanket contract will be retracted, which is what the agent threatened if I don't figure out where the Bennington billion is located."

"The Bennington what?"

"It's a very long story. Can I tell you about it later?"

"Yes. But I can't wait to hear it all."

"Maybe I'll write a book," I lamented.

"If you lose the GM contract, Forward Research and Test will go broke."

"I know that. And thanks for reminding me." Cindy was MBA equipped (with a corporate finance option) and had recently been providing me free advice on how to lease, borrow, or buy the extra test equipment and manpower I'd need to propose significantly expanding Forward Research and Test's role in GM's pre-production test workload. The big auto companies did not take fat-headed risks with little test houses. Thus, I was screwed twice. First, Forward Research was a little test house. Second, financial commitments were already made by my test house to Hewlett Packard and Tektronix to lease and/or buy test equipment, more test equipment than could be afforded under the pending GM-less revenue flow.

In fact, Cindy Salome had demonstrated, with a program from a floppy disk she got in one her MBA books, that unless GM quickly shat (rarely used tense of 'shit') more cabbage (synonym for money), Forward Research would go broke before Labor Day. And it was already June. Worse yet, Beth Drachman's cut, if any, from the pending divorce was undecided. To appear more solvent than I really was, I had overextended my business. It looked bad in every direction. I was approaching a state of high internal anxiety. "Do you have any beer?"

"Are you serious?" inquired my healthier-minded bedmate.

"I am. My stomach is in knots."

"Do you want to talk?" She asked.

I paused. "I do, but not tonight. I need to get some sleep. I've got some numbers to crunch tomorrow."

"It's in the pantry. It's warm."

"I can drink it over ice, like John McEnroe."

"I'm worried about you, Frank."

"It's okay. I'll be okay. Don't worry," I said. And I really meant it. I did not want anybody worrying about me. "I'll get everything straightened out."

But I wanted to know what Ed Finninen was doing with Beth Drachman. That really pissed me off. Ed's innocent 'I'm from the UP eh' bullshit act. Fuck him! He probably worked for the FBI and seduced Beth, the abandoned wife of Frank Drachman, to get information about the Bennington billion. But that would sound paranoid, wouldn't it? Was it that simple? Should I call Beth and ask her? No. How would she know anyway? I had to find that money!

I went to the pantry and found a twelve pack of Old Milwaukee cans. I took two of them and poured one over a tall glass of ice cubes and drank. Then the other. I pondered a while. I stopped to urinate on the return to bed.

"Goodnight," I told her.

"Goodnight, Frank. I'm glad you're here. Are you really all right?"

"Yes, Cindy, I am. Thank you."

She rubbed my clean hair gently and went back to her book. I then fell asleep immediately and slept poorly straight through until morning.

The alarm (Cokie Roberts on NPR) sounded and Cindy and I were off to the races. She showered first since it took her a lot longer to get ready afterwards. This was a common trait among women. We usually showered together on the weekend, but never on Monday. Never. The impending work week required concentration and level setting of mind.

To my pleasant surprise, I had left yet another complete outfit at Cindy's apartment – blue jeans and a pressed red cotton shirt. When did I leave these? I could not recall. The shirt was brand new. I was starting to think that Cindy really loved me or, at a minimum, like to shop. I got dressed and grabbed my bag of evidence.

Cindy wore a gray Anne Klein suit with a yellow blouse (no bow) and black pumps. She looked and smelled beautiful. I wasn't infatuated (bull). We spoke little and jumped into her car. Twenty minutes later we arrived at the doorstep of my failing business. Damn.

"Good luck with your talk today, Cindy. Remember, if you get nervous, picture them taking a crap." I kissed her. Did she look good!

"Thanks, Frank," she started with a smile, "but that approach doesn't work for women."

"Huh."

"Huh yourself," she said nicely.

"Huh me? Huh me? Are you huhing me?" It was my best DeNiro.

"Yes," We stopped.

Then I spoke, "How about if I come by your apartment tonight at seven or so?"

"That's great." She winked at me and was very pretty. I got out of her car and she drove off and left me alone in the small industrial park.

Forward Research and Test was located in Madison Heights in a brand new, shoddily built, industrial park-type building, side by side with three other marginal businesses. There was a subtle competition between the owners of Forward Research and Test (me), T&S Slate and Marble Outlet (Tim and Sheila Patterson), Double-Tite

Rivets (Al 'Bud' Hucholby), and Jeb's Box Outlet (Jeb Wood). Occasionally, we all joked about which of us would be the first to go under. This was still an open question. In addition, Jeb, Bud, and I had a side bet that Sheila and Tim would split up because of their business before any of us went bankrupt. They were constantly arguing about inventory. In truth, I was concerned about losing two wagers.

But it was still early and Andy was not there. Neither were any of my building mates. I found the hidden key above the door to Forward Research and Test and let myself in. A small, receptionistless reception area, backed by a door, isolated the lab area from the outside world. The lab had four test benches along the left hand (when facing the rear of the building) side wall and two PC-equipped desks along the other side wall. Against the back wall on either side of a centered exit door were shelves loaded with useless, important rubble. Overall, the approximately thirty foot by fifty foot lab room looked like I had never left. Papers covered desktops and bench tops, equipment was left out; there was simply a feeling of disarray. Ah, home again! To hell with ISO 9000! Enough nostalgia.

If the threat by Agent Philips was real, then I needed to somehow decode the number string from Arthur Bennington's computer. It did not matter to Agent Philips if I knew what the numbers meant. I was his scapegoat, his means, like I was Gunter Legglar's.

I recalled the numbers from Bennington: 1424679698. Then I invoked the knowledge extracted from Louis Farrakhan's numerology program, which essentially converted the ten digit number steam into a series of possible letters. For example, take the first digits, 1 and 4. This combination of numbers, if associated with letters of the alphabet, could be A and D (1st and 4th letters of the alphabet) or N (14th letter). If 14 represents N, the next numbers, 2 and 4, could mean B and D, or X. The Bennington number pattern only had multiple possibilities for the first four digits since there are only twenty-six letters in the alphabet. Thus, 1424 could only mean ADBD, ADX, NBD, or NX when translated to letters as described above. When combined with the remaining numbers, the following four alphanumeric data strings emerged:

ADBD679698
ADX679698
NBD679698
NX679698

I had absolutely nothing more to go on, but regarded NBD679698 as my best lead since NBD is a well-known bank in the Detroit Area (NBD = National Bank of Detroit). The question was: how could this data translate into some kind of bank account number? I had already concluded that if the original ten digits represented an account number at any legitimate bank, then the FBI would have figured it out and gotten to the money. Also, I concluded that if the FBI had access to the Bennington billion they would leave me alone. These were critical assumptions, made by a fledgling spy, but it just made sense that no federal organization wanted publicity from harassing a civilian, except for the IRS. But that was changing too. Thus, I was left to my own devices to sort out what the FBI could not and assumptions were necessary!

The key assumption was that NBD was the bank of choice of Arthur Bennington. This then meant that 679698 somehow identified an account number. But how? How? Before arriving at my answer, rest assured that I reviewed countless possibilities. Typical considerations: what if 679698 could be multiplied or divided by some other number hidden on the hard drive to yield a ten digit number? What if Bennington simply rearranged the numbers on the hard drive based on some secret non-cyclic permutation? This would mean that several hundred thousand combinations of numbers needed investigation. Overwhelmed, I chose to leave these brute force solutions in the very capable hands of the FBI code breakers. Instead, I would follow the lead that Louis Farrakhan indirectly provided to me. It was simple.

What if 679698 was not a base ten number? Before elaborating further on my theory, a review of number? Before elaborating further on my theory, a review of number bases is appropriate. Let's take, for example, the number two hundred and forty-seven. 274. Note:

$247 = 2 \times 10^2 + 4 \times 10^1 + 7 \times 10^0 = 2 \times 100 + 4 \times 10 + 7 \times 1 = 200 + 40 + 7.$

10 is the number base and the physical location of the multiplier digit indicates which power of the number base the digit multiplies. Take a look at 14 in base ten numbers:

$14 = 1 \times 10^1 + 4 \times 10^0.$

Naturally, the next question is: how could you express the base 10 number 14 (1410) in a different number base, like base 8, for example? How? Like this:

$1410 = 8 + 6 = 1 \times 8^1 + 6 \times 8^0 = 168.$

It then became obvious to me that I should take 679698 and find the number bases which converted it to a ten digit numeric string. My result would be NBD followed by ten numbers. The mystery bank and account number perhaps? Perhaps. Sure it was a shot in the dark, but what did I have to lose?

I sat down at the desk at the rear of the lab and put the bag containing the glass and money in the in the left side drawer. I turned on the PC. It booted up and I double clicked on the Excel icon to get the spreadsheet program going. I constructed an equation to calculate the ten digit numeric strings (i.e. possible account numbers) in Excel-speak that was based simply on number base conversion. What follows is not the actual implementation in the spreadsheet, just the mathematical expression. See Excel user's manual details. Nonetheless:

Account Number = $6 \times N^5 + 7 \times N^4 + 9 \times N^3 + 6 \times N^2 + 9 \times N^1 + 8 \times N^0$.

where N is the unknown number base. After twenty minutes of numerical experimentation, I discovered that 679698 translated into a ten digit numeric string when $44 \leq N \leq 69$. Any integer $N < 44$ yielded 9 digits or less, while $N > 69$ yielded 11 digits or more. Thus, for a ten digit numeric string, $44 \leq N \leq 69$ was required. The actual numbers (taken from Excel):

N	Possible Account Number
44	1016512692
45	1136705813
46	1268009190
47	1411175901
48	1566992312
49	1736278797
50	1919890458
51	2118717845
52	2333687676
53	2565763557
54	2815946702
55	3085276653
56	3374832000
57	3685731101
58	4019132802
59	4376237157
60	4758286148
61	5166564405
62	5602399926

63	6067164797
64	6562275912
65	7089195693
66	7649432810
67	8244542901
68	8876129292
69	9545843717.

I was not done yet, however. As I observed and regarded 679698, reviewed 44 and 69, it occurred to me that there were two other possible account numbers which could be derived from my chosen approach for decoding. The expression,

Possible Account Number = $67 \times N^4 + 9 \times N^3 + 6 \times N^2 + 9 \times N^1 + 8 \times N^0$.

applies for N = 68 and N = 69 only! Do you know why? Because any power of the number base can be multiplied by a number by a number up to one less than the number base. So for base 68 and 69, the first two digits, 67, could, in theory, represent a valid multiplier. The corresponding numbers for this situation:

N	Possible Account Number
68	1435410444
69	1521682883.

I was armed with twenty-eight ten digit numeric strings, derived via an extremely obscure method. Sure the math was correct, but the logic of the choice was nothing better than a guess by an overly left-brained test engineer. It was unconventional, and perhaps the FBI had not thought of it!

The next hurdle was to get more information about the NBD accounts these numbers might be associated with. Should I call Agent Philips and Senator Spectator? Not yet. I leaned too far back in my chair and lost balance. I fell straight back onto the floor and rolled to my left, appreciative that nobody was around to watch. But just as I kneeled to stand up, Andy came in the back door.

"Who's there?" He asked.

"It's me, Andy. It's Frank"

"Frank! My God how are you? It's great to see you. What's going on? Are you still wanted by the police and the FBI?" He walked briskly to me and gave me a fatherly hug.

"Everything legal is fine, Andy. But I've got some other problems with GM contract. They may cancel it." Again focused on business, I looked at my watch. It was a quarter to nine. "I thought we opened at eight?" I said jokingly. "I'm a fugitive for a week and you're slacking off already?"

"No, Frank, no. I stopped at the coffee shop at six-thirty for breakfast, like I do every morning, and I ate. Just as I was leaving, a story broke CNN about a senator who was found dead in his Washington condo, from a small caliber gunshot to the neck.'

'Was it a senator from Pennsylvania?' I asked.

'Matter of fact it was. It was Senator Spectator.'

I almost passed out.

CHAPTER ELEVEN

Most men lead lives of overt desperation; the rest go quietly, but no less desperate.

Richard Chuckens

Andy quietly observed my extreme reaction to the announcement of Senator Spectator's death. We said little after the color returned to my face.

He started to tidy up the lab area. We both had much work to do.

I printed the account numbers, all twenty-eight of them. In the light of the morning's events, I chose to be an optimist, assuming that even with a questionable code breaking scheme, I had found the answer. Sometimes the seemingly impossible was the only choice.

The next task was to get access to an NBD computer, or some other information source, to establish whether or not any of the twenty-eight 'account numbers' were related to the Bennington billion. I thought about Senator Spectator. He seemed like a corrupt but good man. Not too bright, but good. Did Agent Philips know anything about his death? Were Cindy or Beth or my parents in any danger? And what about Wil Porter? I didn't have enough information to know, but I knew who might be able to help- A. Danby Heckman. I decided to call my parents first and tell them that I was no longer a fugitive. It would give them piece of mind Mr. Heckman could wait. I dialed.

"Drachman's," answered my father, as he always did.
"Hello, dad. It's Frank."
"Well, Frankie, how are you? Your mother's been worried. You know that Senator Spectator? We just saw on CNN that he's been killed!"
"I know. I'm...' I stopped my reply in mid-sentence, suspecting ridiculously that their phone, or perhaps my business phone, was bugged. I fully knew, but fully ignored, that if the federal government of this united state, I mean, these United States, really wanted to know something, then it would be known. I clung to illusions. I was scared more then than ever. "I just called to tell you that the Dearborn Police have retracted my arrest warrant. I am no longer wanted for murder."

"That's good to hear, son. Now tell your mother. She's in the office." He covered the phone and I heard his muffled words.

My mother picked up the second phone. "Frankie? Hi, Frankie," she said. "Is it true? You aren't a murder suspect? How wonderful!"

I recalled that only a few years earlier, my parents, along with Beth, had all expressed hopes of my going to graduate school. Perhaps an MBA. Perhaps a master's in engineering. Now, my mother was overjoyed to hear that I was no longer a murder suspect. Expectations had left the building.

"Hi, mom. It's like I told dad, the Dearborn Police have taken me off their list."

"Can you come over for dinner tonight?" Asked my dad.

"And bring your new girlfriend," inserted my mother. "I can show her a hundred new ways to cook frozen chicken breasts. It's more than just a barbecue you know!"

My parents were never this enthusiastic. Who were these people?

"I'd really like to have dinner with you tonight, but I've got a lot to do. Being a fugitive takes its toll on a small business owner. How about in a few days, after I get things settled down?"

"Okay," he said.

"All right," she said. They sounded like discouraged children.

"Oh, by the way, I did a web search and found absolutely nothing in any chat rooms, or anywhere for that matter, about brake troubles on new GM trucks. I've got the latest search engine from Netscape, too. If I can't find it with that, then it's not on the web."

"Nothing?"

"Nothing," she repeated.

"Thanks. I'll call about dinner." We all paused. "Well, I just wanted to update you on my legal status."

"Frankie," said my dad, "I'm still worried about you. This Senator Spectator murder is too much of a coincidence. You know the history books that the married couple wrote? The ones you gave me after grandpa died?"

"Yes," I replied. I was surprised.

"Well, I read some of them, not every page of course, and I'm not the most educated person, but I did read parts of them. What worries me is that as far back as those books go, the people with the power and money almost always won. And I know that when a senator gets murdered, power and money are involved. Do you have any idea what you're up against here? I'm worried about you, just like after the accident with Mike. I've never told you this, but that was not your fault alone, even though you think it was. I just know it."

He searched for more words, while I achieved a new level of high anxiety. Since there was no beer in the lab, I had to ride it out. "Huh." It was the only sound I could make.

"Maybe this should wait until we...," he said.

"No. No Sam," interrupted my mother. "Tell him."

"Tell me what?"

He continued. "I always told you guys to be careful if you were going to drink and never in the car or on the way to school up there in Houghton. Houghton. God only knows who would put a college so damned far away from everything. But the point is that I told both you and Mike to be careful. Not just you, Frank. I told both of you."

"What are you trying to say?"

"Even though we miss him and think about him every day, the way we resolved Mike's dying was that both of you were doing something you really shouldn't have been doing. It was not your fault alone. Mike could have been driving and you could have been killed. Or worse, both of you could have been killed. Chance can be wicked, but you are still alive."

"That was fifteen years ago," I retorted.

"I know that. We want you to know that too. It's like this divorce with Beth. We don't know what happened but it doesn't really matter. If it's over then it's over. What I'm trying to say, Frankie, is that ever since Mike died, you've been carrying around guilt. You don't need to. It's over."

"Huh." It was both comforting and discomforting to be understood in this way. I half desired to tell them that except for a little boredom with each other's life, the biggest problem with Beth and me (see Strunk and White) was caused by selfishness. Plain and simple. But Sam was right. Never mind the details; the Frank and Beth Drachman marriage was over. It was too badly broken.

"That's enough for now, Sam," said my mother.

"Okay, Millie," he said. I knew he knew that she meant business whenever he called her by her first name, Millie. "Son, you call us when you and your new girlfriend, what was her name?"

"Cindy. Cindy Salome."

"Yeah, honey," said Millie. "The two of you can come over for dinner. We understand, so just get your problems with the government sorted out and call us if you need anything."

"Thanks."

"Call me if you need help," he said.

"I'll try. Goodbye."

They said bye at about the same time. Then *click, click.*

I waited for them to hang up first. What a relaxing dinner that will be.

I sat at the desk. My mind reeled. My heart raced. My ankles ached. After a few minutes, I was able to clear my thoughts. I was not prepared to resolve all existing critical issues in my personal life in one mourning. First, I wanted to resolve the mystery of the Bennington billion. Then I could ensure the financial solvency of Forward Research and Test, then I could finish divorcing Beth, then I could get on with Cindy, and then, and then… A pattern was imminent. I could not escape my father's perspective. Andy had finished straightening up the lab and was standing beside me.

"Everything okay?"

"Yup. Can I borrow your car?" I asked after emphasizing the 'p' on the yup.

"Sure." He handed me the keys. Andy drove a 1984 white Pontiac Bonneville. The air conditioning did not work, but the engine always started and always got him home. Andy would never pry into things, but I knew he was curious about the week I was gone, about the blanket contract, and about the dead senator. I liked that he didn't ask many things, but was a very good listener.

"Thanks. I've got to go the bank."

"Oh," he said quietly. I wrote the actual number found on Bennington's hard drive, 1424679698, on the hard copy of the Excel file, folded the piece of paper and put it my pocket. In addition to my decoded account numbers, I wanted to check the obvious, just in case the FBI or NRO had not. It was time to go and see Michelle Brownley-Cartier. Michelle was Mike's high school (and beyond) girlfriend. They broke up when Mike left with me for Michigan Tech. I thought for sure that they would get married eventually. So did Sam and Millie. In fact, they transferred their bank account to NBD because Michelle worked there. Michelle's entire banking career had been at the same branch, which was only a mile or so from my parents' house. The very last thing Mike and I talked about (remember, we had shared several beers in the car, God damn it was that he wanted to get back together with Michelle. All those memories and hopes for Mike and Michelle left a big, sad, empty hole in all of us. I pulled into the parking lot and went into the bank.

There were two people in line and one teller. Luckily, the teller was Michelle Brownley-Cartier. I alternated looking at her (still wholesome and pretty) and the name tag by her window. It had Michelle engraved on it. As I reviewed these and other things, I made eye contact with Michelle and smiled. Even though I wore no name tag, she recognized me immediately. We didn't look much at each other until my turn in line came some moments later.

"Hello, Michelle, remember me?"

"Yes, of course I do, Frank. How are you?"

"Really good," I lied. "My mom told me you still worked here. When did you get married?"

"Oh geez, ten years ago. A long time ago." Time zipped.

I had not seen Michelle in ten years. After Mike's funeral I did see her a few times, but I don't remember where or when. And then, ten years gone! Just like the Led Zeppelin tune.

"Everything fine, I take it?"

"Oh sure. We, Richard's my husband, have two girls - Jackie and Lisa. They're six and eight." Michelle turned a little dual picture frame, filled with side by side wallet photos of two smiling little girls, towards me. The younger one was missing her front teeth.

"They're pretty," I said. I thought about Richard, then Mike.

"Thank you. So, what can NBD do for you?"

"You're not going to believe this, but I need a huge favor. I feel awkward since I haven't seen you in ten years, but Michelle, I honestly have nobody else to turn to." I considered sharing my ostensible connection to the murdered Senator Spectator, but declined my own offer.

She looked at me with concerned, puzzled, yet very affectionate eyes. "What is it?"

"In my pocket I have a piece of paper with twenty-nine numeric strings on it, including the handwritten one, that I think are potential NBD account numbers. I need to know if they represent real account numbers, and if any do, who do the accounts belong to?"

She looked more concerned.

A middle-aged woman came into the bank with her grandson (assumption). He wanted some candy and was irritating.

"I don't know, Frank. I really want to help you but... can we talk after I get off work at three?"

"It can't wait."

A greasy-haired man in a cheap suit looked at me from one of the big shooter desks off to my right.

"He's the manager," whispered Michelle.

I looked at him and crinkled my eyebrows in an attempt to intimidate.

He turned and went back to work.

"I feel terrible about this, but I'm desperate," I said, while looking at her through the Plexiglas.

She squinted her eyes and pursed her lips, then whispered, "Can you leave the numbers here?" Success!

"Absolutely. Let me write my business phone number on it." I removed the folded paper from my pocket (right front) and wrote the phone number for Forward Research and Test, then slid it through the slot on the counter. She unfolded it and quickly scanned the numbers.

"Only a few of these can be account numbers," she said.

I was encouraged. "Which ones?"

"If you include the handwritten one, there are five that start with 14 or 15. That's how NBD accounts are numbered. Checking accounts start with 14 and savings with 15?"

"Michelle, thank you so much. I don't want to get you in trouble, but if there's anything else you can find, as in who these potential accounts belong too, I would be more grateful than you could know."

We both had been whispering and the manager looked steadily in our direction. I did not risk another attempt at intimidation. The child and his grandmother continued to argue about candy until finally he was declared a bad boy and started to cry.

"All right, Frank. If I can. Do you have a fax machine?"

"Yes." She slid the folded piece of paper back through to me and I wrote the fax number on it and slid it back. We smiled and said nothing more.

I left the bank and drove back to the lab, very encouraged.

Inside, Andy was putting the finishing touches on a test fixture.

"Hi, Andy," I said.

"How'd the bank go?"

"Can't say for sure. What's that fixture for?"

"Bill Ball from Medtronics wants us to test their snow mobile speed sensor again. He wants to be double sure that it works in a harsh supply voltage environment."

"Did you remind him that it was tested three times when it was here last time?"

"I sure did, but he said passing voltage transient testing on two separate occasions helped the durability image of the part. Something about a marketing strategy.?"

"Don't any of our customers understand the technical side of testing?"

"I doubt it. Could be the reason they come here." Andy was highly effective at deadpan humor, and at the time I didn't get it.

"Hey," I began, "if Medtronics wants to spend another three thousand dollars on redundant, unnecessary testing for their marketing strategy, who are we to argue?"

"Exactly."

"Anything else?"

"Other than a week's worth of mail and, like you say, possible cancellation of the blanket contract with GM things were pretty quiet while you were gone. What happened with GM?"

"Don't know yet. I decided that it was time to call Burt Morgan and ask him just what the hell General Motors was trying to pull! I was suddenly angry and confident, as if I had just hit the game-winning home run after being summarily taunted by the opposing team. I would trot around the bases and repeatedly remind the infielders that the game was over and ask them if they could see the score board. Problem with that fantasy, of course, is that the only time I had such an opportunity (in eighth grade), I struck out looking. But that was years ago and things had changed! I dialed Burt Morgan's number.

"Hello, Mr. Morgan's office."

"Annie? This is Frank Drachman from Forward Research and Test. Is Burt in?"

"Hang on, let me see if he's available." Annie was Burt's executive assistant (secretary). I was put on hold for a moment.

"Hello, this is Burt Morgan."

"Burt, this is Frank. Frank Drachman."

"Good morning, Frank," he replied.

He either did not know about, or did not wish to comment on, my previous week of excitement. Other than Cindy, Wil, Andy, my parents, and various local and federal law enforcement personnel, I could not be sure who did know. There had been only one local news broadcast proclaiming my state of fugitivity.

"What happened with the blanket contract?"

"I'll get right to it. The procurement people are concerned with your debt to capital ratio and I couldn't get them over it."

"That was never a problem in the past?"

"I understand that, but things change. We have lawyers and accountants running this place now. Not engineers."

"Does the Bagelle ABS module testing have anything to do with this?"

"No, no. Not at all. In fact, we discovered that one of the proving ground mechanic drivers was mad at his foreman, and he fudged three ABS failures in the durability report. I meant to tell you about it sooner, but things have been crazy here. No time to breathe."

"Is this guy on probation? I mean, I dropped everything and went to Arizona because of the report."

"Yes. He was written up and sent home for three days. His union steward has assured us that it won't happen again."

"I feel really confident now," I said caustically.

"I want you to know that the discontinued blanket contract with Forward Research and Test was not my idea. As of last Monday, we have a new executive vice president in procurement, Peter Fleece. He used to be with E-Systems in Florida and he's simply not budging on some of these supplier debt and capital numbers. Not even the non-production suppliers like you. If it were up to me, I'd keep things the same. I like the work you do. It's out of my hands."

I didn't believe him, although I should have. But if he liked my work, why didn't he fight harder with Fleece? "It just seems odd to me, Burt. Really odd. One day my company is approved and the next day it's not." We were both silent. Pause. I continued, "From E-Systems in Melbourne?"

"That's the one," said Burt Morgan. "He was brought in to help manage new relationships with some of the high-tech military suppliers. With smart speed control and the on-board radar stuff that will be coming out on the German and Japanese vehicles, our research and development execs felt that Procurement and Supply needed an experienced leader for the high-tech supply base. Unfortunately, EMC testing is considered high-tech and you just didn't make Fleece's cut."

Burt Morgan was telling me more than required. He might be worth trusting. My mind jumped a track. "Remember Arthur Bennington?" I asked him.

"Yes, of course."

"You were promoted to his old job, right?"

"That's right."

"Have you ever heard the rumor that he was murdered? That his heart attack was not an act of God?"

"What? What kind of nonsense is that?"

"What if I told you that Bennington was caught up in a huge embezzlement scandal involving Dickman Brothers Automotive?"

"I heard about some crazy conspiracy with the Defense Department when he died, but nothing was ever proved. Where did you hear all this?"

"On Dirk Mott's talk radio program," I replied.

"That nut case? I used to listen to him in the eighties, but about five years ago he checked into a mental hospital and spent six months there. Since then, he's been way out there. He thinks everything on the internet is true!"

Damn. I hadn't heard that one.

"Just because he's off center doesn't mean his guests are" I offered in defense of Mott's program. "Have you ever heard of A. Danby Heckman? He wrote a book about the Bennington scandal."

"No, I haven't. Say, Frank, is everything all right? I know divorce can be difficult, very difficult. And just because your blanket contract was retracted, it doesn't mean that your business relationship with GM is over. There's just more paperwork." Now Burt Morgan was worried about me!

"No, Burt, I'm fine, I guess. I'm glad you'll still have at least some of your extra work sent to Forward Research and Test."

"Of course I will. In time, if you can improve your ratios, perhaps we can reinstate the blanket contract. You hang in there. Frank. I've got to run."

"Okay Burt. Thanks for the feedback. I'm looking forward to continued business. Bye for now."

"Goodbye."

Now there's a conversation that will help my business. I was discouraged, but better understood the GM decision. Although I had never heard of Peter Fleece, E-Systems, his former employer, was familiar to me. I pondered and explored my memory...

That's right! A few years ago, E-Systems was the subject of a provocative *60 Minutes* story. Morley and the gang showed some pretty damning evidence which clearly implied that E-Systems was a joint CIA/NO owned and operated military/espionage research and development company. The intelligence community is small and everybody important knows everybody important, regardless of what they say.

Consider the following question: If, from his E-Systems days, Peter Fleece was familiar with the NRO group chasing me for the Bennington billion, would he help them get to me financially? He had vague business reasons to cut Forward Research and Test out of the strategic supply base. His GM subordinates and colleagues did not question it to save their careers. It sounded paranoid, but it made sense.

I noticed Andy working steadily on the Medtronic's sensor. The lab was otherwise quiet. Then the fax machine rang three times. The high pitched beep acknowledged contact between the machines. A one page transmission from Michelle came through. It read:

1 Page Total
Frank, here is what I found

1424679698 - Not a valid NBD account number
1411175901 - Not a valid NBD account number
1566992312 - Not a valid NBD account number
1435410444 - Not a valid NBD account number
1521682883 - NBD account for Foster, Crawford, and Schaefer. Balance = $48,435.18

Foster, Crawford, and Schaefer is a law office, Located at 553 Woodward in Birmingham. A monthly withdrawal of $7,500.69 is the only transaction on record for this account since it was opened seven months ago. The initial deposit was $100,000.00.
That's all I can do! Good luck!

Thank you Michelle! I took the fax and folded it up and put it in my pocket. I still had no wallet. I thought about the twenty-dollar bills that Agent Philips gave me and the glass I took from the jet. I was glad his fingerprints were on them. I thought about my hair, hidden on the government jet. I thought about being able to prove my story. I thought about covering my ass. If this law firm's account was somehow connected to the Bennington billion, then things might fall into place.

I needed the help of A. Danby Heckman, but had no way to contact him. Dirk Mott's radio station might know. For a second I was concerned that Heckman and Mott might have met at the nut house, but that was just my growing paranoia.

"Andy?"

"Yeah."

"I need your car again. I have more errands." I was taking no chances. It occurred to me for the first time (duh) that my lab might be bugged! I was certain they couldn't bug a fax machine, so I was safe there, but phone calls were another story.

"Go ahead. You still have the keys."

"I'll be back in a while."

I drove to a Bob Evans restaurant that was about two miles from the lab. There were payphones inside, near the restrooms, and I considered these to be secure phones. I exchanged two dollar bills for eight quarters with the cashier. I proceeded to the phones and called the AT&T operator to get the number to Mott's radio station, WMES. I knew the radio station's offices were in Southfield. I obtained the number and then dialed it.

"WMES, can I help you?" Answered a friendly male voice.

"Good morning, sir. I am a regular listener to Dirk Mott. A few days ago, Dirk had a guest on his show named A. Danby Heckman, and I read his book called *The Lost Fortunes*. I wanted to talk to Mr. Heckman about a couple of things. I wonder if you have a number where I might reach him?" I spoke formally so as to have just the right amount of nutism in my voice. This would encourage the cooperation of WMES personnel.

"Hold the line, please."

"Sure." I took the shiny phone cord in my left hand (I held the phone ear/mouthpiece with my right hand) and chuckled to myself. I was holding the line. Five minutes passed.

"I'm back. Sorry about the delay. You can reach Heckman at his Detroit office. His number is..."

I stored the number in my brain as he recited it, depressed the lever on the payphone, checked for the dial tone, and called the number.

"Seventy-five cents. Please deposit seventy-five cents?" I complied with the computerized voice and the call was put through.

After a few rings, "Hello, Heckman Associates, Samantha speaking."

"Samantha, my name is Frank Drachman and I need to speak to A. Danby Heckman."

"He's in a meeting. What's this regarding?"

"I have reliable information that could lead to the Bennington billion."

"The Bennington billion? Are you sure?"

"Are you on his research staff?" I asked.

"Yes, I am."

"I'm as sure as I can be. How can I reach Mr. Heckman?"

"Well, if what you say is true, then he's going to want to talk to you immediately. How can we contact you?"

"Please tell Mr. Heckman that I will meet him in one hour inside the Bob Evans restaurant in Madison Heights. It's south of I-696 and west of Mound. One hour. And tell him to bring a camera because I'm not going to give him any originals."

"Okay, all right, I'll tell him right now. But that may not be enough time to get there."

"It has to be," I told her. "It has to be." I hung up the phone, hoping A. Danby Heckman would show. I wasn't wearing a watch, but a wall clock showed it was 10.30 A.M. Before meeting Mr. Heckman at 11.30 A.M., I needed to visit Foster, Crawford, and Schaefer and threaten someone, anyone.

The drive from Madison Heights to downtown Birmingham took twenty minutes. I drove on I-696 west to Woodward, then Woodward north about four miles. At this point, approximately. one quarter mile south of Maple Road on the west side of Woodward, there stands a high-rise apartment building known as the 555 building. The 555 building was so named because 555 was the building address.

Just south of the 555 building, I turned left onto a road (I forget the name) that leads into downtown Birmingham. That's when I discovered the big commotion at 553 Woodward, which is right next door to the 555 building.

Remember those four-door sedans that screeched to a halt by that phone booth just before I was drugged and kidnapped? The law offices of Foster, Crawford, and Schaefer were surrounded by them! I rolled slowly with the traffic, approaching the crowd of people in front of the building. A metered spot opened up a few yards away from the walkway there, so I parked and loaded the meter with one quarter. I had fifteen minutes to look around.

There were several other pedestrians watching from the sidewalk, and strong, silent federal types stood amidst them looking tough. I saw Agent Philips come out the front door. I turned my face away. God only knew how he found this law office. Was I wrong about bugging fax machines?

I became angry and wondered: how can I fuck up his day? I considered my options for several minutes and then returned to the car. I got in and pulled into the street and stopped directly in front of the offices of Foster, Crawford, and Schaefer. I put it in park and got out. Agent Philips was still standing in front of the building. I noticed that the weather was sunny and warm.

"Hey, Agent Philips, AGENT PHILIPS!" I screamed very loud.

He stopped and looked at me through the confusion.

"I've got the goods on you and you don't even know it! You are a dolt!" At the time, I didn't realize how dangerous that man was. I pushed the horn on Andy's Pontiac and yelled obscenities at him. "FUCK YOU! YES, YOU!" I thought fire was going to come out of his eyes, and he broke into a full running stride towards me.

My butt hole tightened and I climbed back into the car. My plan, which was under development at the time, quickly evolved into trying to get him to follow me back to Bob Evans. Wil Porter, computer genius, would have thought it through more carefully than I did.

I sped away, proceeding through red lights. I turned right on Maple, then right again onto Woodward. I raced south towards 1-696 while expertly avoiding several crashes and was impressed with the high speed performance of Andy's car. In the mirror, I saw two federal sedans chasing me. I found it surprising that the Birmingham and Royal Oak Police stayed out of the chase. Good for them.

Once I got to I-696, I slowed down. So did they. In fact, one of the cars stopped the chase and the other, hopefully the one containing Agent Philips, kept within five or six car lengths, but no closer. I drove normally, but mixed it up. I drove slowly, then fast. The sedan never got close to me. The outcome felt unpredictable, but I drove to the Bob Evans restaurant anyway and parked near the entrance and waited. Sure enough, the sedan pulled in and parked next to me. Were they going to kill me? I assumed not.

Without looking directly at them (Agent Philips and some other dummy), I got out of the car and went into the restaurant.

They waited ten or fifteen seconds and followed me. How stupid were they? Didn't they suspect a trap, or were they too arrogant? The latter.

I walked into the restaurant and saw a distinguished-looking man in a turtleneck and sports coat sitting at the counter. He had a camera and a notebook out on the counter, and was apparently alone. I made eye contact.

"Are you Heckman?" I asked.

He nodded yes.

I continued. "Take a picture of the two guys following me. You have to get their faces."

Heckman turned toward the counter to hide the camera. I sat two seats away from him.

Agent Philips and his partner entered.

Mr. Heckman turned and took the picture.

"Nice try," said Agent Philips. "Get the film from that damn thing," he told his colleague.

Mr. Heckman did not struggle.

"Don't let them," I started. "I need…"

And before I knew it, the second agent had taken the film out of the camera and walked out the door. He searched Andy's car without my permission, unlocking the door with a long, flat piece of steel, like the police do.

I went to the window and gave him the finger, and he saw me do it. But I did not go outside; I needed to keep close to Mike Philips, who stayed inside.

"I want to know how you broke the code and found that account," he said firmly.

"What code?" I asked.

He didn't like the humor. He gave me a dirty look and walked out the door. He and his partner drove away.

It all happened so quickly that the lunch crowd in Bob Evans didn't flinch. Didn't even notice. It was strange. I was inside Bob Evans for a total of two minutes and these events occurred. I went back and sat down next to A. Danby Heckman. He exuded calm confidence.

"I'm screwed, you know," I told him.

"How's that?"

"I have evidence on that guy, but without a picture there's no way to reliably trace it to him. He could go undercover, or to another part of the world, and I'd never be able to find him. And it's not like I can chase him around with a camera." Heckman smiled and looked over my shoulder towards the salad bar. He signaled for somebody to come over.

An attractive woman who looked to be in her forties appeared from behind the salad bar, holding a camera equipped with a telephoto lens.

"I believe we can tell you what color eyes those gentlemen have," he said. "Let me introduce you to Samantha Reid."

She extended her hand and I shook it.

"Nice to meet you. Thanks for coming," I said.

She sat down on the other side of Heckman.

"So, Mr. Drachman," he began, "Samantha tells me you were very convincing on the phone, and that you have information about the Bennington billion and the murder of Senator Spectator."

"That's right. It all started after I bought a laptop computer at Arthur Bennington's estate sale. Things were quiet at first, but then all of a sudden I was a wanted man. There's so much to tell. After I heard you on the Dirk Mott program and read your book, I knew it wasn't a coincidence. By the way, what do you think of the overall reliability of information on the internet?"

"Oh, it's quite precise. Quite accurate indeed," he replied.

"Oh yes, very accurate," said Samantha.

"Really?" I added. My second worst fear was just confirmed. I began wondering what I had gotten myself into. However, I still regarded them as my last, best hope. "You wouldn't believe what I've been through in the past week…"

CHAPTER TWELVE

Work diligently, keep silent, and good things might happen. But then again, they might not.

Murray Fritzenhauer

I told A. Danby Heckman and Samantha Reid all about buying Bennington's computer, being carjacked by Gunter Legglar, being followed by that shadow agent with the skinned-up knees (some shadow!), and about the canceled blanket contract and my suspicions about Peter Fleece. I did not tell them how I broke the code. I told them I could prove that I rode on a government jet, but I did not tell them about my hair loop under the seat button. I did not tell them the names of my friends who had helped me. They asked again and again how I broke the code. Finally, I gave them a hint.

"Louis Farrakhan."

They were very puzzled.

I trusted no one, but allowed photographs of the fax after I blocked out Michelle's work fax number with a packet of sugar.

When I took the fax from my pocket, I was careful to pretend that my fingerprints and those of only one other man were on the document. Therefore, only I could touch it. Handling it my way would add to the greater good, I told them. Perhaps I was becoming a liberal.

He offered to dust the fax for prints, but I told him no, that I'd have one of my advisors do it.

"Advisors?" he asked. "Then why do you need Samantha and me?"

"A person can never have too many advisors," I replied.

They asked who the other fingerprints belonged to and I told them.

"They belong to one of the men in Samantha's picture, Agent Philips." Although this was a lie, I could, for the right price, arrange for Agent Philips's fingerprints to be picked up prose the Rob Roy glass I took when I was dropped at Bishop Airport and deposited onto the fax document. I could have the twenties dusted for his prints. Knowledge of Agent Philips's actual prints on paper money could help improve the appearance of the forged prints on the paper fax. I learned of this option in Soldier of Fortune magazine. Shit! I could make up a story about his illegally entering my test lab and trying to steal the fax, because he wouldn't want to admit that he illegally bugged my phone and fax lines. Thank God I caught him, threw him around, and took back the document! How could he argue with this version of the truth?

After all, both of our fingerprints were on the fax! Screw him! We were now playing by his rules.

They also told me that their investigation found it conceivable that Arthur Bennington would use a small, controllable law firm to hide and invest the Bennington billion. Such a firm was paid, probably monthly or quarterly, out of one or more savings accounts which Bennington opened before his death. Foster, Crawford, and Schaefer fit the bill, they said.

It also made sense that Bennington was killed after continuously and stubbornly denying the existence of hidden money, particularly since the Dickman Brothers told all and acknowledged the NO money laundering conspiracy to save their asses, if not their company. One of the Dickman Brothers probably knew that Bennington hid some kind of information on his computer. When this leaked out to the interested parties, the shit hit the fan: sfhaint. The Cuban General sent Gunter Legglar, the NRO sent Agent Philips et al, the British/Canadian/Kenyan governments decided that Great Britain ought to send Agent Hatley to see to the interests of all three. Agent Hatley met Gunter Legglar. Gunter Legglar met Frank Drachman and a concrete wall. Then Frank Drachman met Agent Philips. And whether Agent Philips was FBI or NRO was irrelevant. Very often, Heckman told me, these federal types were members of more than one agency, regardless of what they said publicly. He'd confirmed this from an article he found on the internet.

It was most important to recognize that in the Bennington billion case, they were desperate and reckless. They had already killed three people and hid the truth about them. In fact, Spectator's death was already being reported on CNN as a homosexual lover's quarrel gone bad. A male prostitute was found in Senator Spectator's abandoned car a few miles from Spectator's condo, dead from an apparent self-inflicted gunshot wound. Yes, it was the same caliber gun. That made three deaths: Arthur Bennington, Senator Spectator, and a male prostitute who was, reportedly, also a favorite of Barney Frank's. Samantha believed that Agent Philips and the senator also had a thing going. Based on what I had seen when I was kidnapped, I couldn't argue with her.

In the end, Senator Spectator was killed probably because he wanted to go public with the story, due to some level of internal integrity. Nonetheless, his was a spontaneous, sloppy murder that probably occurred to keep the senator from calling the press or the police in the middle of an argument with Agent Philips or one of Philips's men. Things moved very quickly and I still wanted to control my own destiny. Our conversation waned after an hour.

"I need for you to go on the Dirk Mott show tomorrow and tell the story of the Bennington billion again," I said.

Danby and Samantha looked at each other. I concluded that they were sleeping together.

"I don't know if we'll be ready," he said.

"I don't know if we'll be ready either," she said.

"You have to try. I can tell that Dirk Mott likes having you on the show."

"Oh, I'm aware of that. We go back years," said Heckman.

"Really?" I commented.

"Yes," said Heckman. "We met five years ago during a six-month sabbatical we were both taking."

My worst fear: Danby and Dirk in the nut house together. Confirmed. "Huh."

"I'll call Mr. Mott when we get back," said Samantha.

I shook hands with both of them and we left.

Back at the lab things were very quiet. I went in the front door and walked towards the rear of the building. Where was Andy? Then I saw him sitting blindfolded against the back door! His hands, feet, and mouth were taped with duct tape.

"What happened? Are you okay?" I asked as I removed the tape, first from his mouth, and then from his hands and feet.

"Two fellas snuck in the front door and did this. I didn't even see them! I heard them fiddling around with something and one said, 'I've got them.' Got what, Frank?"

"I'm not sure, Andy. It was probably the two agents in the second car. They probably came to retrieve the surveillance equipment."

"What?"

"It's a long story, but I think the lab phone and fax machine were bugged! They came back to get the evidence." I stood up from a catcher's crouch and Andy got up from the floor.

"Those bastards scared the hell out me."

"Are you hurt?"

"No, just pissed. If those were federal agents and they illegally bugged this building, it just makes me angry. This is not why I fought in Korea. Not at all."

"Let's lock up and take a ride," I said. I recovered the bag containing the glass and money from the desk. Thank God they did not take it! "Do you still have that safety deposit box at your bank, the one for your medals and gold coins?"

"Yes. Sure do. Why do you ask?"

"Would this bag fit?"

"Sure."

"Do you mind if I store it there for a while?"

"Course not. Let's go." We went outside and got into the car. Andy drove.

As he pulled out of the driveway, I asked him something. "Andy, if it meant justice for the two guys that broke into the lab and tied you up, would you sign up to be a witness to something that didn't really happen?"

He became very serious. "You mean justice outside the law?"

"Exactly."

"In Korea," he began, "we didn't take many prisoners and neither did they. I considered that to be justice even though the Geneva Convention said otherwise. What did I see?"

I described the morning's fictitious fax struggle with Agent Philips.

"That's all?"

"That's all. It will probably never come to a hearing, but that's all I need you to confirm if it does."

"Done," he said. We arrived at Andy's bank, which was next door to the Madison Heights Bob Evans restaurant.

I put the folded fax into the bag with the glass and money and kept an eye out for sedans of the federal type. I planned to get those fingerprints transferred very soon.

He went inside with the bag and returned a few minutes later. The clock on the bank sign showed it was 1.11 P.M.

"All set?" I asked.

"That bag is as safe as it can be."

He didn't ask about the contents, but I told him the whole deal. Everything. If anything unusual happened to me, Andy agreed to contact A. Danby Heckman and make sure 'justice' was served.

"I need to go to the Bob Evans to make a phone call," I said.

He drove us there and waited in the car, keeping an eye out for trouble.

I went inside and called my mother. "Hello?" she said.

"Hi, mom, it's me."

"Hi, Frankie. Everything okay?"

"Yes. I need the e-mail address for Senator Spectator, I can't recall what it is."

"But he's dead, isn't he?"

"Yes, I believe the news. But the message is for somebody else."

"Let me go up to the office and check my sent mailbox in America Online for the address." A minute later, she picked up the phone in the office. "Are you ready?"

"Yes. What's the address?"

"aspectator at usasenate dot gov."

"Thanks. I'll call you tomorrow."

"I hope you know what you're doing."

"So do I." I got back into the car and asked Andy to take me to the Kinkos copy center in Warren. It was near the Army Tank Arsenal on Van Dyke and 12 Mile Road. We arrived.

"I'll be out in a minute." I went inside and requested fifteen minutes of Netscape internet time. It cost five bucks. From Netscape I could get to Earthlink, where I had an account with several alias e-mail names. I logged into Earthlink, recalling the password I'd established while angry (bethbitch). Time to change it. Then I wrote and sent the following note to the dead Senator Spectator, knowing Agent Mike Philips, communist, or one of his comrades, would read it first:

To Agent Philips: I am playing by your rules now. You are not smart enough to figure out how I broke the code. Give it up. I have physical evidence that you broke into my lab and tried to steal a fax document. Think hard about how I could have obtained this physical evidence. Given your limited intelligence, you may not believe it, but you should. Just think. Also, I have a witness. I have physical proof that I was on your jet plane. One of my key advisors (A. Danby Heckman - this was not included in the e-mail) *will obtain air traffic records from Bishop Airport by tomorrow morning to corroborate. If you do not tell Peter Fleece of GM to reinstate my blanket contract by the end of this week, I will give my well-known and respected advisor* (Heckman - again this was not included in the actual e-mail) *the information he or she needs to complete the puzzle. If you do not know Peter Fleece, then find an influential CIA friend who does know him. He used to work at E-Systems in Melbourne, Florida. The GM blanket contract must be reinstated, and if anything happens to me, my parents, or my friends, the physical evidence I have described will be made public. I don't want any of the Bennington money. I want my life back with no strings attached.*

PS – Listen to the Dirk Mott program tomorrow if you don't believe me.

The message was launched into cyberspace and I went back to the lab with Andy. We arrived and I proceeded to go through the mail. There was a towing bill for my car from the City of Southfield. It cost four hundred dollars to get my totaled Lumina off the expressway! Who says public service isn't lucrative? Why not charge me for Gunter Legglar's autopsy?

The rest of the day was quiet. At 4.30 P.M., I called Cindy.

"Cindy Salome, body electrical."

"Your body is electrical, babe." I said.

She giggled. "Cindys, did you know that if you mesh your last name's present initial with your first name, you're then plural?"

There was a comfortable pause. "Not until just now," she replied. I knew she was smiling, thinking how odd I sometimes was. I have no proof of this, but was so infatuated with her that I believed I knew her very, very well.

"How did your presentation go?"

"Great. Excellent. All three of them said I did a great job painting the big picture with respect to international standards. They want me to follow up in a couple of months, after I go to Germany! They want me to go to Ford of Germany in Cologne and make a presentation! I can't believe it!"

"I can. Congratulations!"

"Thank you, Frank. Tell me about your day. Do you need a ride tonight?"

"I'm going to have to get a car tomorrow, after I work out the insurance. So, yes, I do need a lift. The other stuff is too complicated to go into now."

"Fine then. I'll pick you up in an hour. If that's okay?" She was irritated that I kept her out of it.

"Maybe we can get some dinner and celebrate your success?"

I suggested.

"Sounds good to me."

"We'll decide where to go when you get here. Goodbye, electron woman."

"Bye, Frank." We hung up.

Andy came over by the desk where I was sitting. "Need a ride anywhere?"

"No. Cindy's gonna pick me up. Why don't you go home, Andyman. I'll see you tomorrow." For some reason I was thinking of Sammy Davis Jr. and his song, 'The Candyman'

"Sounds good. I think I will. You okay?"

"Fine. I'm fine. A little exhausted but fine."

"See you tomorrow," he said.

"Yeah." He left, and the lab was eerily quiet. I went to the front and locked up behind him, still able to smell his Brut aftershave. I decided it was no longer wise to leave the key hidden outside, and retrieved it. When I first moved Forward Research and Test into the building, I figured that since a security guard patrolled the area twenty-four hours a day as part of the building lease, it was safe enough. But I had since changed my position. I went back inside and sat down. It was 4.45 P.M. and I leaned back and started to doze off.

A loud knock at the front door woke me. I went to the door and peeked through the peephole (why not 'peekhole'?). It was two federal-looking types! Shit, damn, hell! Again, there was no need to cuss. In fact, I felt safe. But as an adventure capitalist, trying to become wealthy and find the right woman, I wanted to wonder if I was going to be killed. I opened the door about three inches, blocking it with my foot.

"What do you want?"

"We just want to talk to you."

"Where are your badges?"

They showed them. I realized that if Agent Philips was going to call my bluff and have me killed, I couldn't stop it now. I felt even more calm and opened the door to let them in.

"Mr. Drachman, I'm Agent Stoner and this is Agent Dood. We're from the Detroit FBI office. We received a call from the DC office. The internal affairs people there have been investigating an Agent Mike Philips for some time. He may be involved in very serious criminal activity. The e-mail that we believe you sent earlier today to the late Senator Spectator raised some eyebrows. What physical evidence can place you on an FBI jet?"

"How do I know if I can trust you?"

"You don't. But if we were here for some other reason, would we be asking you to provide evidence which implicates a fellow agent?"

"Probably not." I pulled a piece of hair from the top of my head. "Look under the floor mats on the FBI jet that landed yesterday at Bishop Airport in Flint. You'll find one of these." I handed my hair to Agent Dood and he put it in an envelope. I didn't tell them about the other piece of hair. Just in case.

"What about the other evidence you refer to in the note?" Asked Agent Stoner.

"I'll give it to you when Agent Philips is on trial, when I know that my family and friends and I are safe. Not a minute sooner. I'm not taking any chances. Let me know if you can't find the hair under the mat." They looked at each other.

"Thanks," said the stone-faced Agent Stoner.

"Thanks for your help," said his partner, Dood.

"You're welcome," I replied.

They left.

The lab was again quiet. I was astounded at how quickly things had happened. I sat down and waited for Cindy.

She arrived on time, as always, and we went out for dinner at Tom's Oyster Bar in Royal Oak. I did not talk about my dealings with the federal agents or A. Danby Heckman. I wanted to hear about her successful day. She was chatty. After a two hour dinner, we went back to her place. I did not want to go to my apartment.

"Tomorrow night I have to stay at my apartment," I said. "You know I haven't even been back there?"

"It looked okay when I was there. How about if I cook dinner and stay over?"

"Only if it's pasta and meatballs," I specified, for no good reason.

"Sure. Tuesday is a good day for spaghetti. I'll just come over after work."

"Let's go to bed now," I said.

She smiled. "It's only ten o'clock."

"More time for you know what."

"It's that time, remember?"

I had forgotten. "Darn," I replied. "Those oysters put me in the mood every time. But I am pretty tired."

"Me too." We went to bed and kissed a little and fell asleep very quickly.

Tuesday morning arrived and we were off to the races again. She dropped me at the lab.

Andy was already working when I entered the lab area.

"Medtronics sensor?"

"Yeah. I should finish today," he said. "You need a ride to the dealership?"

"At ten or so." Andy and I carried on with work. I finished going through the mail, paying only the overdue bills. I thought about Beth and our divorce. I didn't even want to talk to her. I needed to call Ben David Fisher and have him call Beth's lawyer to set a date for signing the final paperwork. It was time. Hopefully, Ben David would still represent me since, surprisingly, his firm's intern, Brook Taberman, was not going to press charges. Talk about luck! Cindy had already scheduled her divorce. She wanted to be done with Harry Delrimple. It would be nice to get all that behind us.

I wrote the last check of the morning and looked up to see that it was time to go buy a car. I had purchased my previous three cars from Walt Lazar Chevrolet. He's the perfect, perfect dealer. And, the sales staff knew me. Andy dropped me off there and I shopped for one on the lot. I test drove four vehicles: a Lumina, a Blazer, an S-10 pick-up, and a Camaro. I decided on a black Blazer. After an hour of paperwork and loan approvals, I was on my way.

It was noon. Time for Dirk Mott...

"Welcome to the Dirk Mott program. Today we have A. Danby Heckman with us to discuss the connection between two recent murders: those of Senator Arlen Spectator and Arthur Bennington, respectively the US senator and the retired auto executive, who embezzled over a billion dollars from the National Reconnaissance Office or NRO for short. The ironic part of this story is that the NRO was embezzling the money from you, the taxpayers! Although Mr. Heckman was on this program last week, he asked to be on again today to discuss new evidence about the Bennington billion, which was just provided by a secret witness. It's a small world folks, and big brother is making it smaller! When we return from a station break..."

The aggressive theme song potted up and commercials followed. I did not listen.

Then, "Welcome back listeners. I am speaking with A. Danby Heckman, author of a book called *The Lost Fortunes*. Mr. Heckman just today has decided to delay the publishing of a sequel to *The Lost Fortunes* because of new evidence. Evidence that completes the puzzle surrounding the deaths of two men and a prostitute and the location of one billion illegally hidden dollars. Tell us about it."

"Thanks, Dirk. Yesterday, one of my assistants and I met for over an hour with a secret witness who stumbled upon information leading to the Bennington billion. This man, untrained in espionage, was pursued by agents from several countries and remarkably alluded them all. My sources tell me that the FBI has launched an internal investigation into the activities of at least one of the agents assigned to help the senate subcommittee locate the Bennington billion. You can find more details about the Bennington billion in *The Lost Fortunes*. It is suspected that this agent is responsible for the death of Arthur Bennington and Senator Spectator. My sources also tell me that the Washington DC FBI internal affairs office has located physical evidence aboard an FBI/NRO jet that corroborates the secret witness's story…"

Mr. Heckman told the whole story.

I was going to get my life back! Shortly thereafter, I arrived at the lab, overjoyed. Those two agents were on the level! I went inside and Andy was just answering the phone.

"Oh, wait a minute, he just walked in, Burt," I heard him say.

I took the phone. "Hello, this is Frank W. Drachman." I simply do not know why I included my middle initial.

"Hi, Frank. This is Burt Morgan. I've got some good news. Peter Fleece has agreed to reinstate your blanket contract on a probational basis. It's more of a formality really. He had to do it this way to save face. It just means we review your ISO certification and debt to capital ratio every six months instead of every eighteen months. Everything else is the same. But with the amount of business you'll be getting, it won't even be an issue for long. I have no idea what changed Fleece's mind. Wait until you hear about the work I have for Forward Research and Test…"

I listened to Burt Morgan enthusiastically outline the future good fortune of my company while I slowly faded into thoughts of Cindy and me after dinner tomorrow night. Of course I thought about Beth too, but not that much (bull). I did not think about Ed Finninen (bull). Then I did not know what to think, but I did review all situations in my mind to no real avail. In the end I looked forward to meeting with Peter Fleece to discuss accelerating the reinstatement of my blanket contract.

But first I would have to get a copy of that *60 Minutes* episode about E-Systems so I could study it and prepare. Just in case…

ABOUT THE AUTHOR

Thomas G. Livernois lives and works in the United States.

www.ingramcontent.com/pod-product-compliance
Lightning Source LLC
LaVergne TN
LVHW010201070526
838199LV00062B/4444